Peter and Moira ran to the balcony. They leaned out over the railing and searched the dark landscape below.

"Jack! Maggie!" they called. There was no answer.

"Peter—look!" Granny Wendy was standing by the nursery door staring at something. Peter felt a cold tingling in his stomach. As he approached he saw that it was a piece of paper, pinned to the door by a wicked-looking dagger. The note had Peter's name on it. He pulled it loose and read the strange elegant handwriting:

Dear Peter:
Your presence is required
at the request of your children
Kindest Personal Regards,
JAS. Hook, Captain.

D1081123

Hook

by Geary Gravel

Based on a screenplay by
Jim V. Hart and
Malia Scotch Marmo

and screen story by
Jim V. Hart &
Nick Castle

ARROW BOOKS

Published by Arrow Books Limited
20 Vauxhall Bridge Road, London SW1V 2SA

An imprint of the Random Century Group

London Melbourne Sydney Auckland Johannesburg
and agencies throughout the world

First published by arrangement with Ballantine Books,
a division of Random House Inc.

Arrow edition 1992

1 3 5 7 9 10 8 6 4 2

Text design by Holly Johnson

Printed and bound in Great Britain by
Cox & Wyman Ltd, Reading, Berkshire

ISBN 0 09 913431 4

This
book is for
Ginger and Cliff,
Daniel and Zachary,
Elisha, Nate and Emily,
and, of course,
Sam

"ALL LITTLE CHILDREN, EXCEPT ONE,
GROW UP"

Contents

Hook

1. Play Time

Maggie Banning closed her eyes and lay very still. She was getting ready to be asleep in front of a roomful of people.

This was Maggie's first appearance in a school play, and she wanted it to be a success. After all, the role of Wendy Darling in *Peter Pan* was an important part in a play that was very special to the Bannings. On top of that, her whole family was here to watch her performance. Well, almost her whole family.

Clock chimes began to sound from an old tape recorder offstage as the curtain rose. Maggie opened her left eye the tiniest bit and squinted out into the darkened auditorium.

She could see her mother and her big brother, Jack, sitting up near the front where they said they would be. Next to her mother was an empty seat. Maggie didn't let it bother her. She knew that any minute now her daddy would be there. After all, he had promised, hadn't he?

The clock finished its wavery chiming. Even with her eyes shut tight again, Maggie knew what was going to happen next. A high-pitched squeaking sound told her that the second-grader playing Peter Pan had just flown in on his wire through the Darling family's nursery window. A small thumping sound a moment later meant that he had only stumbled a little when he landed.

A few feet away from him on stage, a wide-awake Maggie Banning lay on the little bed and pretended to be a soundly sleeping Wendy Darling. Holding her breath, she listened to the sounds of a boy looking for his shadow in a bureau drawer.

She remembered from rehearsal that one of the teachers would be following Pan around with a bright flashlight beam that was supposed to be Tinkerbell. She tried not to grin when she heard Pan pull his shadow from the bureau drawer, shutting poor Tink up inside by mistake. *Click* went the flashlight.

There were rustling sounds as Pan made a few halfhearted attempts to stick his shadow back on with a slippery bar of soap. Then he burst into noisy tears.

That was Maggie's cue. She sat up in bed and rubbed her eyes. Taking a deep breath, she said her first line extra loud, to make sure her mom and brother could hear it clearly from where they sat. "Boy, why are you crying?"

The little Pan hopped to his feet and bowed to her. "I'm not crying," he said. "What's your name?"

"Wendy Moira Angela Darling," Maggie recited, taking extra care over the second word. Moira was her mother's name, too. "What's yours?"

"Peter Pan."

"Where do you live?"

"Second star to the right and then straight on till morning. I live in Neverland with the Lost Boys. They are the children who fall out of their prams when the nurse is looking the other way. I'm captain."

"What fun," Maggie said. "Are there no girls?"

"On no," said the little Pan. "Girls are much too clever to fall out of their prams."

Maggie always enjoyed hearing this answer, which made

perfect sense to her. She could not imagine being careless enough to fall out of a pram, which her teacher said was a kind of English baby carriage. She took a step back as Pan spread his feet apart and put his hands on his hips. That was the signal for a big spotlight to come on at the back of the auditorium, throwing his shadow on the wall behind him. The little boy threw back his head and made a loud crowing sound like a rooster.

"Oh, the cleverness of me!" he said.

Suddenly another shadow entered the circle of light. It was gigantic and seemed to swallow up the small figure of the boy. Whispers rippled through the darkened room as people looked around nervously. This wasn't part of the play. Someone—or something—was ruining Pan's big moment!

Along with the other young actors, Maggie squinted into the audience. She saw a man in a business suit duck out of the light and start making his way down the narrow aisle toward the front. He was carrying a raincoat under one arm and a large briefcase in the other.

"Sorry," the man said as he squeezed sideways in front of the seated playgoers. "Excuse me, pardon me. . . ." People grumbled impatiently as he edged past their knees.

Maggie smiled and turned her full attention back to the cleverness of Peter Pan. Her daddy had kept his promise.

Down in the audience, eleven-year-old Jack twisted around in his seat and watched with relief as his father sidled down the row. Sitting through his sister's dumb play wouldn't be so bad now that the whole family was there.

Peter Banning settled himself in the narrow seat and gave his wife Moira a quick kiss. "It was the 'never-ending meeting,' " he whispered. "Traffic was brutal."

"It just started," Moira reassured him.

Peter leaned over to smile at his son. "How was baseball practice, Jackie?"

Jack made a face. "It was okay." He hated to be called Jackie.

"Sit up straight," his father reminded him. Jack sighed.

Moira Banning steered her husband's attention toward the stage. "Your daughter's stealing the show," she whispered.

The three Bannings watched as Peter Pan taught the Darling children how to fly. The most important thing, the little boy explained, was to think lovely, wonderful thoughts. After that it was simply a matter of faerie dust. Little Michael was the first to fly. Then serious John took off, and finally Wendy joined them in midair. The whole audience applauded enthusiastically—well, almost the whole audience.

Peter Banning, investment banker and lawyer, was having a hard time keeping his mind on his daughter's play. He was in the middle of a very important land-development deal that had to be handled just right in order to succeed. If only he had gotten that phone call before he left the office . . . The sound of clapping surprised him. When he looked up, he saw Maggie dangling above the stage on a single slender wire. He jumped to his feet in alarm.

"She could fall!" he cried out. Heights made Peter Banning dizzy, and flying—whether or not it was in an airplane—scared him more than he cared to admit. "How could the school allow them to make a dangerous play like this?" Just watching the soaring children was making his head spin. Behind him parents and children craned their necks, whispering loudly for him to get out of the way.

"It's *Peter Pan*," Moira said, as if that explained everything. She tugged her husband back down to his seat and patted his hand calmly. At her side, Jack was smiling, impressed in spite of himself by the sight of his seven-year-old sister flying through the air.

Up onstage, Maggie gave her family a final wave before soaring through the nursery window after the others. The curtain came down, and the auditorium gradually became quiet again.

Peter Banning sat in the darkness and tried to compose himself. This was supposed to be fun?

Suddenly a high-pitched squealing sound broke the silence. It sounded as if somebody was trying to strangle a cockatoo. Everybody looked around to see where the obnoxious noise was coming from. With a sigh of relief, Peter reached inside his raincoat and pulled out a small portable telephone. Maybe this was the call he had been waiting for.

Moira Banning was upset. "Not now, please!" she whispered to her husband. Couldn't he ever leave the office behind?

People in nearby seats had turned to stare at the Bannings. Jack was extremely embarrassed. He stuck his fingers in his ears and tried to pretend that none of this was happening.

"Brad, make this quick," Peter said into the phone. "I'm with my family. No. Negative—affirmative—definitely. That's why we have an ecologist on staff," he continued too loudly. "Remind him he's not working for the Sierra Club anymore."

Nearby children booed and hissed. Peter Banning slid down in his seat with a guilty look, but didn't hang up. Business was business.

He went on to remind his assistant, Brad, that the Banning

family would be flying to England the following night. Peter was to give a speech at a huge dinner honoring his grandmother for her work with orphaned children. That meant the big meeting would have to be tomorrow morning.

Tomorrow morning! Jack had unplugged his ears just in time. He stared up at his father in disbelief. The big Little League playoff was tomorrow morning. But work always seemed to come first with Peter Banning. "Dad, my game!" Jack protested.

Peter saw the look on Jack's face. "My son's big game is tomorrow morning," he told his assistant. "Got to be there. Yeah, they play in December. It's the Santa series. So let's make it a short meeting—blow 'em out of the water!" He hung up the phone with a satisfied smile, feeling a little bit like a pirate himself.

The curtain rose. The stage had been transformed into a cardboard Neverland. Seven Lost Boys popped out of doorways in seven trees to sing a song about never growing up.

"I wish Peter Pan would come back soon," a little Lost Boy called Tootles said when they were finished. "I am always afraid of pirates when Peter is not here to protect us." Sure enough, a group of second-graders dressed like a raggedy pirate band came onstage dragging a raft. In the raft was a very tall boy made up to look like the fearsome Captain Hook. Soon the Lost Boys were fighting back the fierce onslaught of his marauding cutthroats.

Back in the audience, Peter Banning was fighting back a yawn. It seemed that the more exciting the play became, the less he was able to concentrate. *Peter Pan* was just a silly kids' story, after all, he told himself sleepily. For some reason the tale had always made him uncomfortable with its faeries and crocodiles and flying boys who refused to grow up. How irresponsible, Peter thought. How immature. He remembered Maggie zipping about the stage on her slender wire. How downright dangerous!

Two seats away, Jack was having the time of his life. For a dumb second-grade play, this wasn't half-bad, he thought. His eyes sparkled when Captain Hook challenged Pan to a duel. Of course the old villain lost quickly.

"Who and what art thou?" the pirate cried in wonderment as Pan snatched away his sword.

"I am youth," Pan said. "I am joy! I fly, I fight, I crow!"

Jack nodded, leaning forward. Flying, fighting, and crowing all sounded good to him.

Before they knew it, the final scene of the play was ending—the one in which Pan came back for Wendy one last time, only to find that she had grown up. Her own daughter was now the same age that Wendy had been when the mischievous boy had first appeared in the nursery. It was a sad moment, made a little happier when Pan and his new playmate prepared to fly off to Neverland for another round of adventures.

Then it was all over, and the smiling young actors marched out onstage as the curtain swept closed behind them.

Jack leaned back in his seat and applauded energetically. He looked over at his father, who was clapping along absentmindedly. Jack shrugged. He was feeling too good to stay mad at his dad. After all, Peter Banning had made it to the play as he had promised—even if his thoughts were still mostly back at his office. And tomorrow he would be at Jack's big game.

Jack's mom was applauding proudly in the seat next to

Peter, and there was Maggie bowing and waving up onstage.

Jack smiled and waved back at her. For a while, anyway, the Banning family was together—and wasn't that all that really mattered?

2. Peter's Promise

In Peter Banning's San Francisco office, the big meeting was in its third hour. Peter had just finished telling his staff about his plan to convert a wilderness area into his client's dream of a paradise resort. He told them his strategy for outwitting the environmentalists who would oppose them.

It was a wonderfully clever battle plan. Peter's employees burst into applause. He put up his hands to silence them.

"Let's just hope that between now and the close of this deal no one throws us a curve." Curve? Why did that word seem important? He looked up in alarm. "What time is it?"

"Twelve-twenty," said one of his staff.

The game! Peter rushed out of the office, his employees whirling after him like leaves behind a bus. "My son's going to kill me!" he puffed as he raced toward the elevator. He waved to a tall young man standing in the corridor.

"Jerry?" He knew the guy worked for him, but what was his name? "Jeff?" he guessed. "Jim?"

"Steve," the young man told him.

"I said that," Peter insisted. "Take my video camera. Go to my son's game ahead of me and film what I miss."

Steve sprinted off down the corridor as Peter's staff engulfed him. Everyone had something to ask him or tell him.

Peter slowed his pace as he gave orders and answered questions. Long minutes passed before he finally stepped into the elevator.

A brightly colored banner waved in the wind above the stands: SANTA SERIES THIRD ANNUAL DATENUT LEAGUE WINTER TOURNAMENT. On the field were umpires dressed in Santa Claus suits. The stands were filled with mothers and children.

Jack was up at bat. The scoreboard above the stands read: HOME-8, VISITORS-9. It was the last inning. His teammates were cheering him on. Jack felt nervous but confident. If he could just hit this one . . .

As Jack got ready for the first pitch he looked up into the stands. A man with a video camera was just sitting down between Maggie and his mom. All right! The game was almost over, but his dad was finally here!

For a moment Jack was thrilled, then his heart sank when he recognized Steve, one of the men from his father's office.

"C'mon, Jack," his coach said. "You got one left. Bear down. Stay focused. Keep us alive, Banning, keep us alive!"

The catcher signaled, and the pitcher nodded. In the stands Moira bit her lip. "Please," she prayed under her breath. "Not the curve!"

The pitcher wound up and released the ball. The curve seemed to hang in the air forever. Jack's mind was on his father's broken promise. He swung his bat nowhere near the ball. As it sailed by, the other team broke into a victory cheer. Holding back his tears, Jack walked silently off the field.

3. Peter and Wendy

"Number fourteen Kensington," the cabdriver announced. He began to unload the luggage as the four Bannings climbed out of the taxi.

Peter led the family toward a tall old house. Jack ran ahead, climbing up a steep ledge that ran alongside the steps.

"Jack!" Peter called. "Get down from there! You'll break your neck."

Jack pretended not to hear him. He had barely spoken to his dad on the long plane ride to England. He still couldn't believe his father had sent an employee with a video camera to his big game that morning. By the time Peter himself had arrived at the field, Jack and the others had been long gone.

"Is Granny Wendy really the real, *real* Wendy?" Maggie asked as the family gathered before the huge wooden door. "The one in my play?"

"No," said her father, at the same time her mother said, "Yes." Moira and Peter looked at each other.

"Not really," Peter said.

"Sort of," Moira added. Maggie looked back and forth between her parents, then shrugged.

Peter inspected his family. "Okay, everybody, time to look your best," he said. "Jack, don't slouch. Remember, first impressions are the most important!"

He grasped the ornate metal door knocker and tapped. "Remember, we're in England, land of good manners."

The door swung open, and a sad-looking old man appeared. His eyes were dull, and he seemed to look right through the Bannings.

Peter took a step forward. "Uncle Tootles!" he said.

"It's snowing," the old man remarked. Then he slammed the door abruptly in Peter's face. Jack burst into laughter.

The door opened again, this time slowly. A middle-aged woman dressed in an old-fashioned maid's uniform stood aside to let them in.

"Hello, Libby—Linda? Lisa?" Peter said.

"Liza," the maid corrected him.

"I said that."

Liza beamed at Moira and the children. "Oh, look at you," she cried. "You look wonderful!" The two women hugged.

Moira and the children followed Liza into the living room. Peter stayed behind, looking up the tall flight of stairs. He was beginning to get a queasy feeling in the pit of his stomach. Maybe it was just the plane trip, he thought. The flight over had been exceptionally bumpy. But deep down inside Peter knew that coming back to this place always made him feel strange.

He joined the others in the living room. There were antiques everywhere, along with lots of overstuffed furniture and dozens of old-fashioned photographs.

"Oh, Peter, look at this!" Moira showed him a framed picture of a teenage boy.

"Who's that?"

"It's you."

Peter blinked. He found it hard to believe he had ever been that young.

He heard a noise from the dining room. The old man who had greeted them at the door was down on his hands and knees under the piano. He seemed to be searching for something.

"Lost," he said softly as Peter came into the room. "Lost, lost, lost."

"Lost what?" Peter asked.

"I've lost my marbles," the old man said sadly.

The cabdriver brought in the last of the bags. Peter gave Liza some money to pay the fare. "Please get a receipt," he reminded her in a businesslike way.

There was a small noise at the top of the stairs and everyone turned to see a very old, but very beautiful lady. Peter knew that Granny Wendy was ninety-two years old, but she still carried herself like a young girl. As she came down the steps she looked Peter in the eye.

"Hullo, boy."

Peter could feel himself growing uncomfortable again. "Hello . . . Wendy," he said slowly.

Moira took his arm and led him over to the elderly woman. "I told you, Gran, I'd get him here by hook or by crook," she said.

Peter felt tongue-tied. "I'm sorry it's been so long between visits. . . ."

"It's been ten years," Granny Wendy said. "Now come here and give me a squdge." She gave Peter a big hug, then released him and gave one to Moira. Looking over the younger woman's shoulder, Granny Wendy saw Jack and Maggie come in from the living room. Her eyes grew wide.

"This lovely lady can't be Maggie!"

"Yes, it can." Maggie came up for a hug. "And know what, Great-Grandma? I just played you at school!"

"And don't you look the part!" Wendy turned to Maggie's brother. "Can this giant be Jack?"

Jack stepped back and cleared his throat as if he was getting ready to give a speech. "I'm supposed to tell you congratulations on the opening of your orphan hospital and dedication and . . . stuff." He couldn't quite remember the rest of it.

Wendy gave him a little bow. "Thank you very much."

"You're welcome," Jack said solemnly. He wasn't sure how to act around someone who had lived for almost a century. He walked back to stand by Maggie and his parents.

"There's one rule I insist be obeyed while you are in this house," Granny Wendy said. "No growing up! Stop this very instant!"

The children laughed, and Granny Wendy joined in. She lifted her eyebrow at Peter. "And that goes for you, too, Mr. Chairman-of-the-Board Banning."

Peter gave his head a little shake. "Sorry." He smiled ruefully. "Too late."

Wendy drew back and looked sternly at Peter. "And just what is so terribly important about your terribly important business?"

Jack stepped in between his father and great-grandmother. "When a big company's in trouble, Dad sails in," he explained eagerly. "And if there's any resistance—"

"He's exaggerating," Peter interrupted nervously. "I'm actually still doing acquisitions and mergers. But recently I've been dabbling in land development."

Jack turned to face Granny Wendy. "He blows 'em right out of the water!" he finished proudly.

"So, Peter." The elderly woman gave Peter Banning a look that did not seem to be approval. "You've become a pirate...."

It was early evening. The moon shone down through a break in the clouds above Number 14 Kensington. Snow fell quietly.

Downstairs in the living room, Peter was on his hands and knees searching for a missing cuff link. Nana, Granny Wendy's big English sheepdog, circled him curiously, sniffing at his fancy suit.

As Peter crawled slowly into the large hallway he came face-to-face with Tootles, who was also on his hands and knees.

"I lost my cuff link," Peter told the old man.

"I lost my marbles," Tootles replied.

"I'm not dressed without my cuff links," Peter said, feeling a little silly.

"No happy thoughts without my marbles." As always, Tootles's voice had a touch of sadness.

"If you find my cuff link, would you let me know?" Peter got to his feet with a groan.

"If you find my marbles, would you do the same?" Tootles crawled past Peter and continued on into the living room.

Peter stood at the bottom of the staircase for a long moment. Finally he began to climb the steps. Upstairs, he found himself standing in front of an open doorway. He had an unhappy look on his face. Something had drawn him here, but he didn't know what. A cuckoo clock sounded from inside the darkened room. He took three steps inside and stood still.

He was in the children's nursery. Two beds and a small crib were draped with satin coverlets. On one side of the room was a fireplace with a mantel held up by two homemade wooden soldiers. On the wall was a large mural showing a lagoon where mermaids swam. There were sailing ships in the water, and a tall, red-coated pirate with a hook for a hand stood on one of them. Peter started to back away, then felt the strange pull again. He stepped toward the painting. A chill wind blew past him, and he shivered.

"Peter?" Moira's voice called from outside the room. "Brad's on the phone. He says it's urgent."

The deal! Peter shook himself and ran out of the room. He found Moira in the guest bedroom, holding his portable phone. As he sat down on the bed Jack and Maggie ran into the room. They were playing vampire, and Maggie was yelling in make-believe terror.

"Good news, Brad?" Peter said into the phone. His expression changed. "What? What Sierra Club report? I thought we had these guys. What did they find?" He slumped back down on the bed. "Why is this deal falling apart?" he said with a moan.

Jack took the shade from the bedside lamp and set it on his sister's head. "This will be great," he said. "We'll play shadow warrior." He moved the light to the foot of the bed. Then he started to walk backward. His shadow stretched out like a monster on the wall. "Slowly I turn," he growled.

"Stop it, Jack!" Maggie backed away from her brother. "Daddy, he's scaring me!" she called.

"Shhh . . ." Moira put a finger to her lips and nodded toward their father. On the phone Peter was listening to more bad news. Apparently his whole deal was in danger because of something called a Cozy Blue Owl. He couldn't believe everyone was getting upset just because his development might mean the end of some kind of bird he'd never even heard of. "Ever since the dawn of time, there've been casualties of evolution," he cried. "Ask them if anyone misses a Tyrannosaurus."

"*I* do!" Jack called from the other side of the room. He loved dinosaurs almost as much as baseball!

Peter was trying to control himself. "Are you telling me a five-billion-dollar deal is falling apart because of a ten-inch owl?" he wailed. "Why don't they just go someplace else? Why doesn't somebody just shoot me in the head?"

Jack pointed an imaginary gun at his father from across the room. Peter looked up as Jack pulled the trigger.

"That's it!" he yelled. "Everybody just *shut up* and leave me alone!" He turned to his wife. "Moira, get them out of here. I am on the phone call of my life!"

Granny Wendy was coming down the hall as Moira opened the door and ushered Maggie, Jack, and Nana out of the room. "Come with me," the old lady said to the children, "and I'll show you where your father and I used to stand by the window and blow out the stars."

In the bedroom, Peter had hung up the phone and set it on the nightstand. He ran his hands through his hair and looked up at Moira as she came back to the bedside.

"I never should have come here," he mumbled. "I should have stayed home until the deal was done."

Moira Banning was feeling very angry. "You haven't been

here for ten years, even though Granny Wendy asks you to
visit every year," she said accusingly.

"I haven't had time," Peter protested.

"You promised to spend real time with the kids here, but
you haven't looked at them once, except to inspect them or
yell at them," she told him. Her voice was soft, but steady. "I
mean, how many more broken promises will there be, Peter?"

Just then the phone began to squeal. Peter reached auto-
matically toward the nightstand. "It's Brad," he said. "I've got
to take this call. I've got to fix this."

Moira shook her head. "You've got to fix your family
first." She picked up the squealing phone and tossed it right
out the window. Peter's mouth fell open.

"Your children love you, Peter," Moira told him. "They
want to play with you. How long do you think that lasts? Soon
Jack may not even want you to come to his baseball games. We
have a few special years with our children and then it's over."

Outside, Nana the dog lifted her head as she heard something fall with a plop into the snow. The portable phone was
making tiny squawking noises as she walked over and sniffed
it suspiciously. She barked into the mouthpiece a few times.
Then she walked over to a patch of bare snow and began to
dig. When she was done, she picked the phone up carefully in
her teeth, carried it to the hole she had made, and dropped it
in. Then she buried it under several inches of dirty snow.

4. Panic!

Jack was bored. He looked out through the big windows in the nursery and listened to tunes on his CD player. Outside was a small balcony with a sturdy iron railing. The windows were half-open, and he could feel the cold, snowy night that waited just beyond the room. He glanced over his shoulder.

On the floor in the middle of the room, Maggie sat with Granny Wendy under a tent made from a sheet. They were using a flashlight to read together from a ragged old book. The title on the front of the book was *Peter Pan and Wendy*.

"You know where faeries come from, don't you, Maggie?" Granny Wendy asked her great-granddaughter. They read the answer out loud together: "When the first baby laughed for the first time, the laugh broke into a thousand pieces and they all went skipping about—that was the beginning of faeries."

Faeries! Jack snorted in disbelief. He pushed the head-phones tighter against his ears and turned back to the open windows.

The book that Maggie and Granny Wendy were reading had a faded illustration of a young girl. She was standing in her nightgown next to the open windows of a nursery. The name "Wendy" was written under the picture. "Look," Granny Wendy said. "That's me. It was a long time ago."

Maggie was puzzled. "But Jack says you're not really the *real* Wendy."

Granny Wendy had a twinkle in her eye. "See where Jack is now?" she whispered. "That is the very same window. And this is the very same room where we made up stories about Peter Pan and Neverland and old, scary Captain Hook."

"Really?" Maggie gasped.

"Really. Sir James Barrie was our neighbor. He loved our stories so much he wrote them down in a book." Granny Wendy paused. "Dear me, that was over eighty years ago."

Maggie was impressed. "Boy, Granny," she said. "You're the oldest person I've ever known except for my dad."

Peter Banning himself appeared in the room at that moment. He was nervously checking his watch. It wouldn't do for Granny Wendy to be late for her own testimonial dinner. He walked over to the tent and stuck his head inside.

"Maggie, honey, Granny Wendy shouldn't be late to the most important event in her life." He helped Granny Wendy up off the floor.

Maggie jumped to her feet, gathering the tent up into her arms. "Daddy, I made something for you. Next time you fly, you don't have to be scared." She held up the sheet. Ribbons had been sewn around its edges.

"She's made you a parachute," Granny Wendy said.

Peter patted Maggie on the head and hung the tent parachute on a bedpost. "That's very thoughtful, dear," Peter said. His mind was still on the time. Glancing over to the open windows, he saw that Jack was standing up against the little iron railing. "Jack!" he cried. "Get away from there!" He dashed across the room and snatched his son back from the balcony. He was very upset. He slammed the windows shut and locked them each securely. "What have I told you about playing near open windows? I want this window kept closed for our entire visit!"

Jack got into one of the small beds. He felt like a baby, and that only made him angrier. He pulled his baseball mitt out from under the pillow. "Hey—where's my special baseball? It was right here!" He looked suspiciously at his sister.

"The mean, scary man at the window stole it," Maggie said quietly.

"There is no scary man," Peter said sternly.

Moira came into the room and helped Granny Wendy tuck Jack in while Peter put Maggie into her own small bed. He felt sorry he had been so gruff. She was only a little girl, after all. "Tuck yourself in the envelope of your sheets now," he told her. "And mail yourself off to Dreamland." When Maggie asked him for a stamp, Peter gave her two kisses. "Overnight special delivery," he said.

Then he walked over to the other little bed, where Jack lay pretending to be asleep already.

"Faker," Peter said. He took out his gold pocket watch and handed it to his son. "I'm only going to be gone a couple of hours," he said tenderly. "Here's my special watch so you can keep track of the time."

Over in the other bed, Maggie asked her mother not to go out. She wanted her parents nearby tonight, though she wasn't sure why. Moira sang her a lullaby to calm her. Before the three grown-ups left the room Granny Wendy turned on the small lights above the children's beds.

"Dear night-lights protect my sleeping babes," she said softly. "Burn clear and steadfast tonight."

The children snuggled down into their beds. Even Jack had to admit he felt a little safer now.

An hour later, both children were sleeping peacefully. Maggie was lying sprawled crosswise on her little bed, while her brother was buried under his covers. Above them the tiny night-lights suddenly glowed brightly, then just as suddenly winked out.

Shadows began to creep up the nursery walls in the moonlight. Jungle trees and sharp jagged rocks appeared and grew larger, as if a faraway island was slowly moving closer and closer to the Darling nursery. A big dresser in the corner of the room suddenly started to glow with a greenish light. Its two big mirrors looked like the dark eyes of a skull. Then the room was filled with a creaking sound like that of a ship tugging against its anchor. A wooden rocking horse started to buck all by itself as if someone was riding it, and a cold draft of wind blew out of nowhere. Everything went black for a few seconds, then strange sparkling lights began to shine just outside the big windows.

Down below, Nana tugged at her chain as she looked up at the darkened house. *"Hoof! Hoof!"* she barked, sounding very much as if she was trying to speak.

In the den Uncle Tootles was asleep on the couch. He woke up as the wind beat hard against the doors. He stared at the fireplace mantel, where a tiny pirate ship rested inside a bottle. "Hook!" the old man screamed. "Hook! Hook! Hook!"

The doors burst open, and a chill wind swept into the room.

By the time the fancy Rolls-Royce delivered Granny Wendy, Moira, and Peter home to Number 14 Kensington, they were all relaxed and laughing. The dinner had been a huge success, and Peter's speech had gone well. It was the first time in many years that he had felt so good.

"I didn't do too badly, did I?" he asked Granny Wendy as he helped her out of the car.

"I think it was a wonderful evening," the old woman replied. Then she stopped and looked up at the tall dark house.

The front door was open, moving slightly in the cold wind. With a gasp of alarm, Peter dashed up the stairs. A deep gash had been cut into the thick wood of the door, as if something very sharp had been scraped along it. Peter stuck his head inside the quiet house. "Hello?" He tried the light switch. Dead. He ran to find some candles. He was beginning to feel afraid.

Moira came into the hallway. "Liza?" she called in a trembling voice. "Tootles?" No one answered.

Peter handed his wife a candle just as Granny Wendy joined them in the hall. "Good God!" the elderly woman cried. "The children!"

"Maggie! Jack!" Peter led the way up the tall staircase. The candlelight flickered on a deep, ragged gouge in the wallpaper.

Nana stood at the top of the stairs, a piece of broken chain around her neck. She whined frantically as if trying to explain what had happened. She seemed to be guarding the crumpled form that lay on the floor at her feet. It was Liza. As Peter, Moira, and Granny Wendy crowded around, the maid woke up. There was a big bruise on her forehead.

"The door hit me," she sobbed. "And the children were screaming—"

The children! Peter ran to the nursery. The big door was shut. He opened it and charged into the darkened room.

It looked as if a hurricane had hit. Furniture was upended, and toys had been thrown from one side of the room to the other. The little beds were empty. Lace curtains flapped eerily in the big open windows.

Peter and Moira ran to the balcony. They leaned out over the railing and searched the dark landscape below.

"Jack! Maggie!" they called. There was no answer.

"Peter—look!" Granny Wendy was standing by the nursery door staring at something. Peter felt a cold tingling in his stomach. As he approached he saw that it was a piece of paper, pinned to the door by a wicked-looking dagger. The note had Peter's name on it. He pulled it loose and read the strange elegant handwriting:

> *Dear Peter:*
> *Your presence is required*
> *at the request of your children.*
> *Kindest Personal Regards,*
> *JAS. Hook, Captain.*

At that moment Uncle Tootles walked into the room. "Have to fly!" he said in a raspy, cackling voice. "Have to fight! Have to crow! Have to save Maggie! Have to save Jack! Hooky's back!"

Granny Wendy collapsed to the floor.

5. Pixie Power

The police arrived quickly. Bright lights flashed out front from several cruisers and an ambulance. Inside the house, men were working to restore the electricity.

When the police inspector found out who Granny Wendy was, he thought the kidnapping might just be a prank. After all, there couldn't really be a pirate named Captain Hook who went around stealing children, could there?

Later Peter and Moira sat at Granny Wendy's bedside. The old woman was still weak after her fall. "There's nothing we can do now but wait," Peter told her. "The police are doing everything they can to—"

"The police can do nothing," Granny Wendy interrupted. She asked Moira to get her a cup of tea. As Peter rose to help his wife Granny Wendy asked him to stay.

"Don't worry, Gran," he said. "I won't leave you."

She didn't answer until her granddaughter was safely out of the room. "Ah, but you always did, every year," she said then. "You don't remember that. Every year you returned to me, remembering nothing, and every year you left me again."

"Take it easy, Gran." Peter was worried. It was obvious that the evening's shock had taken its toll on Granny Wendy. "Maybe you shouldn't try to talk."

Wendy knew what he was thinking. "I'm not crazy," she

assured him firmly. "Peter, what has happened to your children has to do with who and what you are."

Peter was bewildered. "What are you talking about?"

Granny Wendy asked him to hand her the worn copy of *Peter Pan and Wendy* sitting on her nightstand. She opened the book to the first page.

" 'All children, except one, grow up,' " she read. She looked up at Peter. "That's how Sir James began the story he wrote for me, such a long time ago. It was Christmas, in the year 1910, and I was almost eleven. A girl becoming a woman, caught in between two chapters. How far back can *you* remember, Peter?"

Peter was feeling sick and dizzy. He wasn't in the mood to play this game with Gran. "I remember the hospital in Great Ormond Street. You worked with orphans. You taught me to read. You arranged for my adoption. . . ."

"But you were already twelve, nearly thirteen," Granny Wendy said. "What about before that?"

"Before that . . ." Peter tried to think back. "There's nothing," he said.

"Think hard." Granny Wendy was staring at him with a determined look on her face.

"I was cold. . . ." He thought for a while longer, sweat beading on his forehead. Finally he gave up. "I can't! No one knows where I came from. You told me I was a foundling."

Wendy nodded. "That's right. *I* found you. Half-frozen to death on the windowsill of the nursery of this very house. It was the year you came back for good, fifty years too late."

"Fifty years?" Peter was really worried now. Granny Wendy was talking nonsense. The shock of the children's disappearance must have been even greater than he'd thought.

"Peter, you must listen to me now," Granny Wendy told him. "I was an old lady when I wrapped you in blankets, already a granny, with my thirteen-year-old granddaughter Moira asleep in the nursery. And when you saw her, that was when you decided not to go back to Neverland."

Peter's mouth fell open. "Go back *where*?"

"To Never-Neverland, of course," Granny Wendy repeated as if it were obvious.

"Moira!" Peter yelled. This was proof that Gran had lost her mind. He stood up. "I'm going to get Moira."

"Peter, I have tried so many times to tell you." Granny Wendy looked more determined than ever. "I could see you had forgotten. I knew you would think I was just a silly old woman. But now I *must* tell you!" She reached out and pressed Peter's hand against the old book, speaking rapidly. "The stories are true, I swear it to you. And now Captain Hook's come to seek his revenge. The fight isn't over for him, Peter. He wants you back. He knows you'll follow Maggie and Jack to the ends of the earth and beyond—and by heaven, you must find a way. Only you can save your children. Somehow you must go back—you must make yourself remember." She shook her head. "Oh, Peter—don't you know who you are?"

She held up the book and showed him the famous illustration of a young boy standing with his feet apart and his sword drawn. He had his head thrown back as if he was just about to crow.

Feeling sick, Peter Banning stared blankly at the picture.

That night Peter could not fall asleep. Instead of going to bed, he went up to the empty nursery. The great windows still stood open. As Peter walked toward them he noticed the parachute Maggie had made for him hanging on the bedpost. He picked it up, then let it flutter silently to the floor. He stood at the railing and looked out into the starry night. Then, closing his eyes tight, he lowered his head and began to cry.

After a while a cold breeze stirred the lace curtains. Peter opened his eyes.

One of the stars had fallen out of the sky. As he watched in amazement it began to hurtle toward the house. Was it a meteorite? he wondered. Or maybe a satellite falling out of orbit? He gasped as it came nearer and nearer. Oh my God, he thought. It's a low-flying plane, a *very* low-flying plane! It seemed to be heading right for his window!

He backed away from the railing. A second later the light burst into the room. It was tiny! It flew around Peter's head in circles like a firefly.

"You're kidding," Peter said to himself. The darting light blazed and sparkled with energy. It flew around the room, knocking pictures off the wall as it went. "It's some kind of bug," Peter muttered. He rolled up a magazine and followed the thing, swatting at it in the dark room. Then the light turned and somehow snatched the magazine out of his hands. The next thing he knew, it was swatting *him*! As he backed away he stumbled over the edge of the baby crib and sat down in it with a plop. The tiny light dropped the magazine and lowered itself gently to the desk. There was a flash of bright light.

Peter stared. A tiny girl stood there—she couldn't have been more than six or seven inches tall. As he watched she walked toward him, stepping through an open inkpad on the desk before she marched right up the front of his chest. Her feet left tiny prints on his clean white shirt.

Miniature wings sparkled on her back as she hovered nose to nose with him. She sniffed his face.

"Oh, it *is* you." She had a tiny voice to match her size. "A big you." Still floating in the air, she folded her arms. "I guess it's not bad that you're big. You were always bigger than me—maybe this means you'll be twice as much fun."

Peter was terrified. He hunched his shoulders up around his ears and tried to call for help. All that came out of his mouth was a weak whisper. "Moira . . ."

"Oh, Peter, what fun we'll have again!" The tiny girl did a somersault in the air in front of his face. "What times, what great games!"

Peter gulped. He pulled his glasses out of his pants pocket and put them on upside down, his hands shaking. He squinted at her.

"You're a—you're a little faer—" he started to say.

"Faerie," she finished for him.

"A pix—a pix—"

"Pixie." She cocked her head to one side. "And if less is more, there's no end to me, Peter Pan."

"Peter Banning," he corrected her.

"Pan."

"Banning."

"A fat, old Pan!" she insisted.

"A fat old Banning!" he said.

She shrugged. "Well, whoever you are, you're still you." She sniffed again. "Only one person has that smell."

"Smell?" Peter was a little insulted. He had showered twice today.

"The smell of someone who's ridden the back of the

wind," the little creature told him. "The smell of a hundred fun summers sleeping in trees, having adventures with Indians and pirates." She darted back and forth in front of his face until his glasses fell off. "Oh, remember, Peter—the world was ours and we could do *anything*!" She came close enough to brush his face. "Ow!" she cried. "Whiskery things!"

Peter pried himself up out of the crib. "It's finally happened," he muttered to himself. "I'm having a total nervous breakdown."

The little pixie grabbed Peter's bow tie and pulled him toward the open windows. She was surprisingly strong for such a tiny thing. "Follow me," she said, "and all will be well."

Peter tried not to trip over the dollhouse on the floor. "Where are we going?" he asked.

"To save your children, of course. Captain Hook's got them, and you have to fight him." She waved her left hand, and a shower of shimmering dust fell on his face. "Let's fly!" she cried.

Peter's only response was to sneeze loudly. The force blew the faerie out of the air and right through one of the windows of the dollhouse. Peter got down on his hands and knees and examined the little house as all of its windows suddenly lit up.

"It's true then." The little voice came from inside the dollhouse. "You did grow up. The Lost Boys told me, but I didn't believe them." She sounded very sad. "You used to call me Tink." Peter thought he heard her sob. "Have you forgotten *everything*?" she wailed.

He slipped his glasses back on, right side up this time, and peered into the dollhouse.

"Are you in there, little bug?" he asked.

Tink was infuriated. "I'm not a bug!" she yelled. "I'm a faerie."

Peter shook his head. "I don't believe in faeries," he said.

Tink was horrified. "Every time someone says 'I do not believe in faeries,' somewhere there's a faerie that falls down dead."

Peter was starting to feel overwhelmed. He had had enough of this talking hallucination. *"I do not believe in faeries!"* he shouted. He heard a loud crash. He lifted the hinged roof of the dollhouse and found Tink lying sprawled dramatically at the bottom of a tiny staircase.

"Oh God," he said. "I think I've killed it!"

"Clap," Tink whispered, her eyelids fluttering. "Clap your hands, Peter. It's the only way to save me."

Hesitantly, Peter brought his palms together.

"Clap, Peter, clap!" Tink cried. "Louder. *Louder!*"

"I'm clapping, I'm clapping," he said, feeling ridiculous.

Tink hopped to her feet and brushed off her tunic as Peter's clapping gradually ran out of steam. She wandered into the dollhouse kitchen, where a Barbie doll was preparing to serve dinner to Ken. Tink sniffed in disapproval and rearranged the figures so that Ken was waiting on Barbie. "All right now," she said to Peter. "Who am I? I know you know."

Peter would not give in to a hallucination, even if it could talk. He tried logic. "You're a psychosomatic manifestation," he told the pixie. "A composite of all the girls and women I thought I was in love with in my life." He got to his feet and dusted off his palms. That was telling her!

Tink shot out of the dollhouse and flew to the end of the rug Peter was standing on. Reaching down with her tiny hands, she gave the carpet a great tug. "Guess again," she said as Peter did a double backward flip in midair. He hit his head with a thud on the hardwood floor, sprawling limply on his back on top of Maggie's parachute. He pointed to the empty air above him. "Look—stars!" he said weakly.

"That's right, Peter." Tink picked up the ribbons Maggie had sewn onto the sheet and wrapped the makeshift parachute around him. "Second star to the right and straight on till morning!" She pulled the ends of the ribbons together and hovered over his bundled body. *"Neverland!"* she cried.

Tiny wings flapping in a blur, Tink lifted Peter off the floor and carried him out through the nursery window into the cold night air. He was much heavier than she had remembered, and she struggled to stay aloft, looking like a miniature stork on her way to deliver a decidedly overgrown baby.

Peter twisted and murmured inside the para-sheet. "My back . . ." he complained.

"Not *your* back," Tink corrected him. "The back of the wind! We'll catch it if we hurry."

Big Ben was starting to chime midnight as they soared into a starlit sky. As they passed over a couple kissing good-night under a street lamp, Tink shook out a little of her faerie dust. Still kissing, the couple rose slowly into the air, their eyes closed and their heads filled with happy thoughts.

6. Pirate Town

An unconscious Peter floated gently down through layers of fluffy clouds. Somehow Tink had managed to strap him into the para-sheet's harness. She flew beside him, her eyes on the remarkable view of Neverland below them.

Surrounded by ocean on all sides, Neverland was a mixture of craggy mountains and hidden valleys, snowy peaks and tumbling waterfalls. Mermaids played in a lagoon not far from the patchwork settlement known as Pirate Town. Just off the coast of the main island rose the Nevertree. Taller than any redwood, the mighty tree reached toward the sky from its own small islet, safe from irate Indians and pillaging pirates alike.

Tink beamed with delight. She was returning home to her beloved Neverland with the greatest hero of all in tow! At her side, Peter Banning began to snore quietly.

When Peter woke up, he was lying underneath Maggie's sheet. Above his head, a tiny sword began cutting an opening in the whiteness of the sheet. Tink dropped down, swinging on a ribbon.

"Ahhh!" Peter screamed when he saw that his hallucination had come back to haunt him. "You!" He jumped to his feet, pulling off the sheet.

Peter stood and stared in disbelief. He was in the middle

of a town square like none he had ever seen before. All around him were buildings made out of old ships. People dressed in colorful costumes were hurrying to and fro. Noise and dust were everywhere. In the center of the square stood a huge stuffed crocodile. It must have been at least thirty feet tall. Wooden scaffolding had been built around it to hold it upright, and it held a big broken alarm clock in its nasty-looking jaws.

"What is going on here?" Peter turned around in a slow circle. "Where am I?"

Tink rolled her eyes. When was he going to get it? "Neverland," she said.

"Neverland," Peter repeated unbelievingly. He took a few steps out into the square.

"No! Get under cover!" Tink beckoned to him from under the sheet. "Peter, what are you doing?"

Peter felt his forehead. "I need an Advil," he said. He checked for his portable phone under his jacket. It was missing. "Excuse me," he asked a passing pirate. "Is there a pay phone around here?"

"Get back here!" Tink sputtered. "Get down, get low! Hide! Stop!"

Ignoring her, Peter walked to a ladder that led down to a building on a lower level. A big sign nearby said SOUP KITCHEN. Tink flew after him.

"I'm still dreaming," Peter muttered to himself as he walked. "A very vivid dream." He pointed toward Tink. "I've got it. I'm at the dentist. I'm on nitrous oxide. I'm having my teeth cleaned, and you're the dental assistant. Nurse, I want to wake up right this instant!" he insisted.

Tink hovered over Peter's hand. Her tiny sword slashed downward. A tiny streak of blood appeared.

Peter yelled in pain. "That's so unfair of you—why did you do that?"

Tink looked apologetic. "Oh, Peter, I hated doing that. I hated it." She handed him a pint-sized handkerchief. "I would never, ever harm you. But this *is* Neverland, and you are *not* dreaming." She flew up in front of his face. "Now who am I? Say it!"

Peter started to wrap the hanky around his hand. "I can't say it," he told her.

"Why not?"

"If I say it, you're real."

Tink was determined. "Say it, Peter. You have to say it."

"You're Tinkerbell!" Peter blurted out finally. Then he shook his head. "No," he said. "I can't accept this. This is not rational adult thinking."

"Adults think," Tink reminded him. "Children believe."

Peter walked away from her. He stood facing the huge Croc Tower. "If I'm having an actual conversation with a seven-inch flying faerie," he said, "then I'm insane. Peter Banning is *not* insane."

Tink was getting frustrated. "We have a lot of work to do," she told Peter. "You're going to need your sword, and you're going to have to fly."

"I don't fly," Peter reminded her. "And I'm certainly not going to fight this Hook person with a sword." He walked to the front door of the soup kitchen. "I'm going to sit down and discuss this with him like a rational adult."

"But you're not ready!" Tink cried. "And you won't get very far dressed like that."

Peter marched into the ramshackle soup kitchen. The place was filled with pirates in colorful rags. They began to gather around the strange man in the elegant suit.

"Gentlemen," Peter said politely, "maybe you could help me. I'm looking—"

"If it ain't a pretty little penguin!" one pirate interrupted. He seemed to have no teeth at all. "I fancy them shiny boots." Other pirates began to lay claim to different parts of Peter's clothing.

Peter looked around at the burly men with their swords and pistols. He was finally beginning to realize the danger he was in. He turned to run from the soup kitchen. The gang of pirates blocked his way.

"Tink, *help!*" he cried.

"Don't get no blood on them boots," the toothless man warned his comrades. "They're mine!"

Peter spotted Tink hovering at the edge of the crowd. "If you're really Tinkerbell, help me!" he pleaded.

Tink smiled in satisfaction. At last he had admitted who she was! She streaked to Peter's side.

"Mess with him and you mess with me!" the tiny faerie cried. She picked up a pirate and heaved him out the window.

Peter could hardly believe it. Tink zoomed here and there, throwing pirates through the windows with ease. As she got rid of them she collected pieces of their clothing, which she brought to Peter one by one: torn pants, a wide hat, a cape. Finally she gave him an eye patch, which he stuck over one side of his glasses.

"If you insist on seeing Hook and desire to be alive when you do so, do exactly as I say," Tink told him when his disguise was complete. She was hiding under his hat. "Your right arm is dead and hangs at your side. Crack your mouth and drool."

Peter did his best to follow her instructions. Tink inspected him. When she was satisfied that he would pass for a pirate, the two began to stroll through the dirty, busy streets of Pirate Town.

Peter looked in amazement at the pirates all around them. Tink headed them toward a pier at the edge of town, where a large sailing ship was anchored. They passed a blacksmith who was grinding something on a metal wheel. Sparks flew in the air. Nearby stood a short, fat man with spectacles perched on his round face. He held a fancy-looking red pillow. As Tink and Peter watched, the blacksmith used tongs to drop the piece of metal onto the pillow. It had a red-hot point at the end of its curving shape. Peter blinked in surprise.

It was a hook!

The fat man left the blacksmith's and started off toward the pier.

"Follow that hook!" Tink whispered to Peter from his hat. The two of them hurried off after the fat man. They had to struggle to keep up in the crowded streets. The fat pirate made many stops along the way. He led them in and out of a barbershop where pirates were having their hair cut. He stopped at a shoeshine stand to have the hook polished. Next he went into a tavern for a mug of beer. Pirates joined him at every stop. "Hook! Hook!" they chanted.

At last the procession reached a dark tunnel. Peter saw a sign near the entrance:

HOOK VS. PAN

Near the sign a man was selling tickets. "Hook versus Pan!" he called out. "The ultimate war! See the boy fly; see the boy die!"

Peter and Tink were swept into the tunnel with the crowd of pirates. At the end of the tunnel was the long pier, and at the end of the pier sat the ship called the *Jolly Roger*. The back of the ship was shaped like a skull and had two big windows that looked like eyes. A wooden plank went from the pier to the ship. The fat pirate led the way as Peter and Tink were pushed up the plank along with the rest. The fat man opened a door to the cabin of the ship and disappeared inside. Hundreds of pirates milled around on the deck. "Hook! Hook!" they chanted. "Show us the hook!"

Peter shrugged. "I've done business with the Japanese," he bragged to Tink. "How tough could this be?"

The little pixie was not so confident. She flew out of Peter's hat and hid herself behind a bottle on top of a nearby barrel. She wanted to be ready in case Peter needed her.

The fat pirate had come back out of the cabin. He climbed down the steps to the deck and lifted a megaphone.

"Good mawning, Neverlaaaand!" he called to the assembled pirates.

"Good morning, Mr. Smee!" they shouted back.

"Tie down the mainmast, maties," Mr. Smee said. "Here he is, the cunning kingfish, the bad barracuda, the sleaziest sleaze of the Seven Seas, and a shipshape dresser to boot!" The pirates laughed as Smee took a deep breath. "A man so deep he's nearly unfathomable; a man so quick he's even fast asleep!" Smee climbed back up the steps to the cabin door. "Let's give him a big hand, because he's only got one!" The pirates laughed harder than ever. Smee lifted a finger and shushed them. He pointed at the cabin door. "I give you the steel-handed stingray—Captain James Hook!"

"Hook! Hook! Hook!" The pirates cheered and danced around.

The door to the cabin swung open. Captain James Hook walked out to greet his men.

With his bright red coat and his big black hat, Hook was the perfect example of a pirate leader. He had a long nose and a thin black mustache, and his eyes burned with a crafty cruelty. His left arm ended in a sharply curving hook made of gleaming, glistening silver.

The pirates applauded wildly.

"See how greatly the men favor you, sir!" Smee said close to the captain's ear.

Hook had a big smile on his face. "The puling spawn!" he snarled. "How I despise them."

Peter watched the captain from the back of the pirate crowd. "That's Hook?"

"You cut off his hand and threw it to the crocodile," Tink whispered hopefully from behind the bottle. "Remember, Peter? Is any of this coming back to you yet?"

Peter was feeling more and more confused. "No," he said, nodding yes at the same time.

He watched as Hook sentenced a pirate named Gutless to spend time in something called the boo-boo box. After the screaming man was locked inside, the pirates opened a small door in the box and dropped in spiders, scorpions, and one fierce-looking snake. Peter shuddered.

Hook addressed the rest of the men. "Prepare to kill youth, destroy joy, and strangle innocence!" he told them.

Peter decided he had had enough of this foul man. It was time to sit down and discuss the release of his kids. "I'm going to go find out where Jack and Maggie are," he told Tink.

The pixie was horrified. "Wait, Peter!" she cried. "He'll kill you. You're not ready yet!"

"It's going to be all right," Peter assured her. "He's the one who should be afraid. After all—*I'm* a lawyer!"

Hook was too busy lecturing his men to notice Peter at the back of the crowd. "Peter Pan is coming soon!" he promised them. "I shall have my great war, *and I shall win!*"

At his signal a net was hoisted up from the ship's hold. Two small captives huddled inside the net.

Hook smiled at them. "Hello, children," he said. "Comfy? Cozy?"

Peter stared in shock at the children. "Jack! Maggie!" he cried. Peter couldn't bear to see his kids hung up like fish in a net. He pushed his way to the front of the crowd and ran toward the children. Jack and Maggie were overjoyed to see him.

"That's my daddy!" Maggie cried. "Fight, Daddy, fight! Get us out of here and take us home!"

Dozens of bloodthirsty pirates drew their swords. Peter was suddenly surrounded. Two of the pirates grabbed his arms.

"Let go of me! Those are my children!" he yelled, struggling desperately.

Tink sat cross-legged behind the bottle, shaking her head. "I told you so," she said.

"C'mon, Dad," Jack shouted. "Blow 'em out of the water!"

"It's all right," Peter reassured his son. "Daddy's handling this." He turned to face Captain Hook. "Do you have an attorney?" he asked. "I'm the father of those children and I want them down from there. And lower them gently!"

Hook stood still as a statue. "Who are you?" he asked in a quiet voice.

"I'm Peter Pan—Banning, I mean. And I'm an attorney-at-law, and those are my children. I want them back."

"Those are your children?" Hook said. His shifty eyes looked back and forth from Peter to the young captives. "And you're—"

"Peter."

Hook almost laughed out loud. This middle-aged, over-weight codfish? "Smeeee!" he called over his shoulder. "Who is this imposter?"

"Peter floggin' flyin' Pan," the first mate said. He brought out a stack of papers. "I've got a description of him right down to his toenails—a sworn document signed by a Miss T. Bell."

Peter was as surprised as Hook by this announcement. "I am *not* Peter Pan," he said loudly.

"I've got his medical history," Smee said. "I've even got dental records. He may look like a fat slob, but he's Peter Pan."

Smee handed the captain his reading glasses. "Put them on and I'll show you something," he said. Consulting his papers, he undid Peter's shirt and pointed to a scar on his left side.

Hook gasped. "The hypertrophic scar."

"Right where you sliced him up during the Tiger Lily incident," Smee confirmed with a nod.

Peter had never heard of a hypertrophic scar. "That's my appendix!" he said.

"Your appendix is on the other side," Smee reminded him. The final proof came when Hook noticed the tiny footprints Tink had left on Peter's shirt.

"Faerie tracks! He's Peter Pan," Smee swore, "or I've got a dead man's dinghy."

Hook looked almost sad. "It *is* you," he said to Peter. "My great and worthy opponent. But it can't be. Not this pitiful, spineless, bloated, pasty codfish I see before me. You're not even a shadow of Peter Pan." He turned and walked away.

Peter cleared his throat. "Gentlemen, I think we have an obligation to clarify this massive misunderstanding. I want my children."

Hook looked back at him sorrowfully. "I want my war," he said.

"Then I think we have some room to negotiate," Peter said. He was beginning to feel more comfortable.

"Negotiate?" Hook repeated the word as if he had never heard it before.

"Yes," Peter said. "In plain English, to find a middle ground, to cut a deal."

Hook reached for a sword when he heard the word "cut."

"I didn't mean that literally," Peter said hastily. "You have something, I have something, and we find some middle ground."

Hook shook his head. It was time to make things clear. "*We* have something," he said. "You, however, have nothing."

Hook threw the pirate sword. It sailed between Peter's legs. *Thud! Twang!* The sword buried itself in the wooden leg of the pirate standing right behind him.

"Fight me!" Hook challenged. "Fight me with all the cleverness of the true Pan and win your children back!"

"I can't fight you." Peter looked hopelessly around the pirate ship. "I don't know how."

"Oh, rubbish." Hook didn't believe that for a minute. "Pick up your weapon," he said.

"All right . . ." Peter put his hand on his back pocket. The pirates stepped back nervously, grabbing their own weapons.

Suddenly Peter whipped out—his checkbook! "How much?" he asked as he started to fill out a check.

Hook's mouth hung open. *This* was Peter Pan's weapon? "Oh, you poor man," he said. He picked up an old-fashioned pistol and fired. The bullet grazed Peter's checkbook. Then it ricocheted to the side and struck a plump pirate with a white apron. The man toppled over backward.

"Who was that, Smee?" Hook asked.

"Sid," Smee said. "The cook." The pirates all cheered. Apparently the cooking aboard the *Jolly Roger* had needed some improvement.

Hook began to walk toward Peter. Peter backed up as Hook forced him toward the steps to the upper deck.

"We haven't explored all the options," Peter stammered. "Let's work together on this. You have prime waterfront real estate crying out for development!" He fell backward onto the bottom step. "I just want my kids," he said.

"And I just want my hand," Hook replied. "There are some things in life you just can't have back. But, true to my glorious good form, I am willing to give you the chance you never gave me." He looked over at the net holding Jack and Maggie. "Hoist them! Raise the kiddies!" he bellowed to his men. "Hang 'em high!"

Pirates manned the crank. The net went higher and higher into the bright blue sky. "I'll make you a deal, Mr. Chairman of the Board," Hook said to Peter. "Fly up there and touch your frightened children, and I will set them free."

Peter stared helplessly up at his children, so far above him. He gulped. "I can't fly."

Hook was amazed. "You can't fly? Then climb, crawl, or slither up there, Pan. Be yourself!"

"I'm afraid of heights," Peter whispered to Hook.

Hook and the pirates began to laugh. Peter Pan afraid of heights? "Now I've heard everything," the captain said. "Get up there! Move!"

"Save us, Daddy!" Maggie called. "I want to go home!"

Peter took a deep breath. "It's all right, Princess," he called. "Hang on, Jack. Daddy's coming."

He grabbed hold of the rigging and started to climb. "Someone give me a hand," he puffed. He was not used to this kind of exercise.

The captain held his gleaming hook up into the sunlight. "I already have," he said with a smile.

Sweat trickled down Peter's brow. The higher he got, the harder it was to keep climbing.

"Touch their fingers and this will all be just a bad dream!" Hook called from below.

Peter reached the yardarm. Now he was only a few feet from the kids. He started to crawl out on a narrow beam of wood. Finally he stopped, too afraid to go any farther. Behind him, a pirate sneaked up the rigging. He threw a rope around Peter's ankle and tightened it.

"C'mon, Dad!" Jack called to his father. "You can do it!"

"Just reach out," Maggie said. "Touch my fingers, Daddy, and we can all go home!"

"Don't give up!" Jack shouted. He was stunned. How could his father act like such a coward? "They're going to kill us—don't you care?"

"Daddy, save us!" Maggie was starting to cry.

Down below, the pirates made fun of the children. They called up to Peter in baby voices.

Hook wore an expression of disgust. "I cannot soil my steel with your blood," he said to the terrified Peter. He signaled to the pirate standing in the rigging under Peter. The pirate gave Peter a shove that toppled him from the yardarm. Down he fell. Pirates rushed to catch him.

Hook addressed the crew. "Gentlemen, I'm afraid that I have decided to cancel the war."

The pirates groaned in disappointment.

Hook gave the order for Peter to walk the plank. The pirates dragged him to the narrow board. He stood there on wobbly legs, still dizzy from the climb and the fall.

"He ruined my beautiful war," Hook said. "Kill him. Kill them all. And I never want to hear the name 'Pan' again." He struck his hook on the railing and headed toward his cabin.

Suddenly there was a streak of light. Tink appeared hovering in front of the captain. "What about the name 'Hook'?" she asked. "Is this how you want to be remembered? As a bully?"

He slashed at her with his hook. The pixie dodged him easily. Hook's hook stuck in the wall of the cabin. He yanked at it, trying to pull it loose. Tink flew up in front of his face. She stuck the point of her tiny dagger against the end of his nose. "One week and I'll get him in shape," she promised with a prod to his nose. "One week and you can have the war of the century. Your whole life has been building to this moment. Mortal combat—glory—Hook versus Pan!"

With his free hand, Captain Hook pointed to the plank, where Peter was trying to keep his balance. *"That* is not Pan!" Hook roared in disgust.

"Seven days is nothing to a man as important and powerful as Hook," Tink said.

The flattery seemed to work. Hook leaned in closer to the hovering faerie. "Three days," Hook countered, finally wrenching his hook loose from the wall. "My final offer."

"Done!" Tink reached out her tiny hand and shook the hook.

"You'd better deliver, Miss Bell," Hook threatened, "or no amount of clapping will bring you back from where I'll send you."

Peter began to inch his way back up the plank. Thank goodness that part was over!

When Hook announced that the glorious war would take place in three days, the pirates cheered and waved. The man standing nearest to Peter put out his arm and knocked Peter off balance. There was a loud splash. Everyone rushed to look over the side. "Oops!" said the pirate.

Peter had sunk quickly out of sight. Tink hovered anxiously over the water. "Can't you really fly, Peter?" she called. "Then you'll have to swim! You can swim, can't you?" Tink was afraid the worst had happened. Tears in her eyes, she flew off above the ocean.

Underwater, Peter was sinking like a stone. His lungs felt as if they were about to pop. Just as he was blacking out, a beautiful face appeared in front of him. A mermaid! She took Peter in her arms and gave him a big kiss. Suddenly he felt that he could breathe again—even though he was still underwater! Another mermaid came up and kissed him, then another. Soon he wasn't drowning anymore. Two of the mermaids grabbed his arms and began to tow him away from the *Jolly Roger*.

7. Pursuit

Breathing underwater made Peter even dizzier than climbing the mast. When he came to his senses, the mermaids were stowing him inside a giant clamshell. One of them put a rope in his hand and showed him how to pull it. They each gave him a farewell kiss. Then they vanished in a swirl of seaweed.

A pulley was attached to the rope. As Peter tugged on it the clamshell rose up out of the sea and kept on rising. Finally the clamshell stopped, tipped over, and Peter fell out. Suddenly there was snow falling. Peter slipped and slid down a small hill, running into a group of penguins. Just as suddenly the snow was gone and he had stopped sliding. There were summer flowers all around him. A flock of pink flamingos hurried past him. Peter's head was finally clearing. He looked around.

He was on a great upthrust of rock. In front of him was a vast island with mountains and forests. For a moment he wondered if whoever owned it would consider selling any of their land. Then he turned and stared at the immense tree that towered behind him. It looked as if it had been growing for thousands of years, and its highest branches seemed to graze the clouds. Around the base of the tree the land was divided into areas that seemed to represent the four seasons; Peter saw a green and springlike section that gradually blended into a

golden summery landscape. Beyond that were the bright leaves
of autumn, and then the snows of a gentle winter.

"Where am I?" he whispered. He took a step forward, and
suddenly a vine closed around his ankle. He was hauled off his
feet and hung upside down. His keys and credit cards tumbled
out of one pocket and fell past his face. Loose change and
some breath mints fell from the other pocket. Huffing and
puffing, Peter tried to reach up to the branch the vine was tied
to.

On the branch was a tiny little house made out of a clock.
Inside the house Tinkerbell lay sleeping on a bed made from
a seashell. Suddenly the house shook. Tink fell out of bed. Was
it a treequake?

Outside, Peter was shaking the branch that held the house
as he twisted and turned. He was beginning to hate hanging
upside down. "The blood's rushing to my head," he groaned.

Tink heard Peter's voice and came flying out of her house.
She was overjoyed when she saw him. "Oh, you're alive!" she
sang.

Peter wasn't sure if he was alive or not at this point. "I'm
upside down," he told Tink, as if she couldn't see for herself.
"And very high up in the air. Please get me down. I believe in
you. I really believe!"

Tink zipped back into her house. A moment later she
walked out onto the tiny porch. In her hands were a pair of
little gold sewing scissors. "You'll need the Lost Boys," she
said. "They can do anything! We've got to make them believe
you're Pan. Then you'll get your kids back, I promise!" As she
spoke she snipped away at the vine that held Peter's ankle.

Peter noticed what she was doing. His eyes grew wide.

"No!" he yelled. "Don't cut—that's not a good solution! Wait! Listen! *Don't cut!*"

At that moment the vine gave way. Peter hurtled downward. He bounced once, twice, then hit the ground. "Oh, my aching back," he moaned. Then he looked around. After all, he *was* alive.

In the meantime, Tink had gone to spread the word. She flitted like a bee through the gigantic Nevertree. "Pan's back!" she cried.

The Lost Boys were in the middle of their afternoon nap. Tink zipped in and out of their treehouses, calling out the news. One by one they came out, blinking sleepily. Soon more than twenty of them surrounded Peter. He had never seen so many ragamuffin boys before. Most of them were holding bows and arrows. Peter backed away nervously. Behind him, a barrel rolled down the hill. Before he knew it, the barrel smacked into the backs of his legs and knocked him down. The Lost Boys set the barrel upright again. It broke open to reveal a very large Lost Boy with a big belly. He looked at Peter, who was still covered with vines and leaves. "Who's the shrub?" he asked.

"Bangarang!" yelled another one of the boys. They all charged Peter with their knives. Luckily, they only wanted to cut away all of the leaves. Then they stood back to look at him.

"That ain't no Peter Pan!" claimed one. He had the very strange name of Don't Ask.

"He's old," said No Nap.

"He's fat," added Latchboy.

"He doesn't looks so fat to me," said the very large boy, whose name was Thud Butt.

"He's an old grandpa man," said Too Small (who really was).

"Pardon me?" Peter said. He might be a little overweight, and he might be middle-aged. But he certainly didn't feel like anyone's grandpa!

"What would Rufio say?" Ace wondered. The Lost Boys nodded and looked around. Where was Rufio?

Suddenly there was a loud crowing sound from the top of the hill. "Rufio!" cried all the Lost Boys. Their leader was here.

The boy was dark-skinned. He was dressed in ripped black trousers and his black hair was streaked with bright red. He had a sword in one hand, and he was riding on a windcoaster, which was a bit like a skateboard, but bigger. It had a mast like a ship and a large sail made from lots of different-colored rags. The boy started down a steep slope. Halfway down, he suddenly jumped onto a low-hanging trapeze. He twisted around, hung by his legs for an instant, and grabbed a nearby vine.

Peter was horrified. "This is so dangerous—he could fall!" he said to little Don't Ask. "How does he get down from there?"

Then he found out. Rufio swung back and forth on the vine, let go, and twisted into a double flip. He landed right in front of Peter.

Peter was shocked. Dressing up in clothes from the secondhand store was one thing. Running around on slippery ground with pocketknives was much more dangerous. And doing somersaults off a vine with a sword in your hand . . .

It was more than Peter could take. He had children of his own, after all.

"Okay, son, you've had your fun," he said to Rufio. "Now put that thing away before you poke somebody's eye out.

That's a dangerous weapon!" He looked around for support from the others. The Lost Boys stared at him silently. "Where are your parents?" Peter fumed. "Where is an adult?"

Tink was hanging in Thud Butt's slingshot as if it were a swing. "You're forgetting where you are!" she yelled to Peter. He was going about this in exactly the *wrong* way.

Peter ignored the tiny voice. "I want to speak to somebody in charge!" he demanded.

The Lost Boys all turned and pointed at Rufio, who took a deep bow.

Peter shook his head. He had no intention of wasting any more time with this reckless kid. "I want to speak to a grown-up," he insisted.

"All grown-ups are pirates," Rufio said.

"Excuse me?"

"We kill pirates," Rufio told him. The Lost Boys nodded in agreement.

"Well, I'm not a pirate," Peter said. "It so happens I'm a lawyer."

This did not seem to be the right thing to say. "Kill the lawyer!" Rufio yelled, charging forward. Peter gulped and ran for the tunnel, the Lost Boys at his heel. Peter froze in shock as the boys fired their bows and arrows. One—two—three—four!

"I've been shot!" Peter yelled. Then he looked down at his body. The arrows were hanging from his shirt and pants. He pulled at one. "What is this—glue?" Peter was disgusted.

He dashed toward the tunnel as two Lost Boys who were twins started after him.

"He married Wendy's granddaughter, Moira!" Tink yelled at them. She zoomed along the ground and pulled up a vine.

It stretched between two trees. The twins tripped and fell flat. "Hook kidnapped his kids!" She turned in midair and flew by another group of boys. "He's just out of shape! We have to get him back in shape!"

The boys looked at each other in bewilderment. What on earth was this mixed-up pixie talking about? Rufio shot past Peter on his windcoaster, knocking him to one side. He sat down in a field of flowers, trying to catch his breath. Some of the flowers leaned over and sniffed at him. Peter jumped to his feet. What kind of backward place was this?

He ran around a corner and got a big surprise. The Lost Boys were waiting for him. They shot another volley of arrows at him. One caught him square on the backside. The arrow bobbed up and down as he ran away. The boys stopped to argue how much the shot was worth. One of them had a chart listing all the points.

Tink grabbed the chart and tossed it away. "Stop! He's your captain! He needs us!"

The Lost Boys looked at the funny-looking man running with the glue-arrow stuck to the seat of his pants. "Him?" they asked Tink.

The faerie flew after Rufio and tugged on his jacket.

"Rufio, you're the best with a sword. Teach him," she pleaded. "We have to help him remember!"

The other Lost Boys had gotten out their skateboards and set out after Peter. As they were catching up, one of them slipped. His skateboard shot out from under him just as Peter jumped in the air to avoid another arrow. All of a sudden Peter was on a skateboard! He zoomed forward, waving his arms.

"How does this thing stop?" Peter yelled as a wall appeared in front of him. He skated straight up the wall and went sailing off the skateboard. Somehow he landed on his feet right beneath a basketball hoop. The skateboard came down through the hoop and landed in his arms.

The Lost Boys started a wild skateboard basketball game with Peter in the middle.

"Play!" Don't Ask ordered, throwing a basketball to Peter. It bounced off Peter's stomach. The Boys crowded around as he watched them helplessly. Peter slipped and fell to the ground with a loud crash as the Boys scored basket after basket.

"Bangarang!" the Lost Boys shouted.

The boys stood back as Rufio swung down on a vine toward Peter, his sword raised to strike. Peter jumped to his feet. There was no place to run. This was it! At the last minute Rufio laid his sword sideways on the top of Peter's head. "You're dead, Jollymon," the dark-skinned boy said triumphantly.

Peter was confused. He certainly didn't feel dead.

"If you're Pan, you got to prove it." Rufio circled Peter as the other boys watched. "Can ya fly?"

"Fly, fly, fly!" the Lost Boys chanted hopefully. A few hopped up in the air to show him how to do it. Peter stood still.

"Can ya fight?" Rufio asked. The Lost Boys handed Peter a heavy broadsword. Peter tugged at it. It was too heavy for him to lift off the ground.

"Help!" he shouted as Rufio raised his own sword. "Somebody dial nine-one-one!"

Rufio shook his head in disgust at the phony Pan. "Last question, Pops. Can ya crow?"

At last something he could do! Peter took a deep breath.

He threw his head back and opened his mouth. Then he made a sound like a sick canary.

The Lost Boys howled with laughter. Rufio gave a proper "king of the roost" crow. He spun on his feet like an ice skater. Then he kicked the sword out of Peter's hand.

Tink had had enough. She flew up in the middle of the boys. "Silly asses!" she scolded. "I could have told you he can't do any of those things! He doesn't even remember how to play simple games. And now Hook's got his kids, and I've got *three days* to get him ready to fight! And I need everybody's help!"

The Lost Boys were astonished. "Peter Pan's got kids?" one of them said doubtfully.

"He's got a family, he's got a mortgage, and he's got a few extra pounds," Tink told them. "But he's still our Pan!"

Rufio had his own idea. He drew a line in the dirt with his sword. Then he stepped to the other side of the line. "He can't fly, he can't fight, and he can't crow. Whoever thinks he ain't Peter Pan, come cross this line."

That sounded sensible to Peter. He leaped across the line and waved to Rufio. "Hi!"

Tink grabbed Peter by his suspenders and jerked him back over the line.

"You're embarrassing me, you silly ass!" Tink said. She let go of his suspender. It snapped him hard in the back.

The Lost Boys had reached their decision. One by one, they crossed the line in the dirt. Soon all of them were standing next to Rufio. Well, almost all of them. Little Pockets was still on Tink and Peter's side. He reached up and tugged on Peter's shirt. Then he pulled the tall man down until their heads were on the same level. He stared hard into Peter's face. There were lots of wrinkles around Peter's eyes, cheeks, and mouth. Was there a Pan in there? Pockets put his fingers on Peter's face and started to smooth out all of the funny lines. He pulled Peter's forehead until it was all smooth. Then he gave a big gasp.

"Dere you are, Peter!" Pockets exclaimed. He talked as if he had a head cold. He grinned at the other Lost Boys. "I found him!"

Several of the boys crossed over the line and crowded around. They wanted to believe this was Peter Pan. They pushed and poked at Peter's face.

"Peter, is that you?" Latchboy asked. "Why did you grow up? You promised never to grow old!"

"Welcome back to Neverland, Pan-the-Man," Too Small said with a smile.

"Wow—his nose got real big," Don't Ask said.

Rufio would not give up. "Don't listen to that stinkin' faerie," he jeered. "I've got the Pan sword, and *I'm* the Pan now. This guy can't take it from me!"

What Rufio said made sense. Ace, No Nap, Thud Butt, and Latchboy stepped back over the line to Rufio.

"No, wait!" Little Pockets said. "If Tink b'leeves he's Pan, mebbe he is."

The boys considered this. The same four crossed back over to stand by Peter.

"Ha!" Rufio sneered. "You gonna follow this drooler to fight Captain Hook?"

Rufio had a point. Latchboy, No Nap, Ace, and Thud Butt went back over to their leader.

"Whad's he doin' here if he's nod Pan? He don' look happy to be here. Who are dose kids Hook stold? Gib him a chance!" Pockets said.

Peter straightened up. He knew one thing that was true.

"Those are my children, and Hook is going to kill them unless we do something." He spread his hands. "Help me, please!"

Little Pockets looked shocked. Peter had said the "P-word"!

Tink had been sitting on a nearby lantern. She flew into the air to get the boys' attention. "When Pan's away, you always ask: what would Peter do?"

The pixie was right. What would Peter Pan do? That's what the Lost Boys should be doing right now.

"I know!" Ace said. "He'd get the Lost Boys back!"

Peter looked at the group of ragtag boys. "But aren't *you* the Lost Boys?" he asked.

"Yeah, but there's more than this," Don't Ask told him. "Hook catches lots of us when we're not looking. Then he shoots us out of cannons!"

"He makes the little ones crawl the plank!" Too Small added.

Peter thought that sounded like a very mean thing to do to a little boy.

"We're afraid to rescue them without Pan," No Nap told him.

"Even Rufio," Too Small added in a whisper.

Rufio was scornful. He didn't like to admit he was afraid of anything. "It's survival of the fittest," he said. "We're better off without the slow ones."

Peter tried to think. Since arriving in this strange place, he didn't know what was happening anymore. But he did know one thing. He'd do anything to save his children! "If I have to crow, I'll crow," he told the boys. "If I have to fight, I'll fight. If I have to fly . . ." He hesitated. "Well, maybe I could *run*, real fast."

Tink flew down to sit on his shoulder. Her eyes sparkled with hope. "Believe your eyes," she told him. "Believe in faeries, and Lost Boys and three suns and six moons. Find one happy thought and hold on to it. What used to make you happy will make you fly." She touched his cheek. "Will you try, Peter?"

Peter looked around him in the deepening twilight of Neverland. High up in the Nevertree, pink, white, and blue faerie lights were beginning to glow. The sky was alive with sunset colors, and the littlest Lost Boys were starting to yawn. If all of this is real, Peter thought, was the rest of my life a dream?

"I'll try, Tinkerbell," he said.

8. Plots and Pans

It was nighttime in Pirate Town. Lights blazed from the *Jolly Roger*. In the captain's cabin, Hook and Smee paced back and forth in front of the two huge windows. From the outside, the windows looked like two big eyes looking nervously from side to side.

Hook was having doubts about his bargain with Tink. "What have I done?" he moaned to Smee. "I have agreed to an absurd war, and now I am bound to wait for Pan's return." He pounded his hook on the desk. "And what am I waiting for?" he asked himself. "Whether it's three days or three years, he'll always be a fat, old Pan."

"How about a bit of music, Captain?" Smee asked. Maybe that would take Hook's mind off his troubles. Smee unscrewed the hook from his captain's arm, replacing it with a freshly sharpened one. Then he attached the first hook to a record player and lowered it onto a record. Soft music filled the cabin.

Hook didn't seem to notice. "I hate being disappointed," he whined. "I hate living in Neverland. I hate being alive, and I hate, hate, hate, hate, *hate* Peter Pan."

"Let's go play with your war toys, Captain," Smee suggested. "Show me your strategy." He walked over to a wonderful little scale model of Neverland set in a tub of water. "C'mon, Captain, you've got all your pirates and your Indians and Lost Boys. And here's your favorite boat." He pointed to a tiny version of the *Jolly Roger*. "Come on and play with me, Captain."

Hook was depressed. Even pretending to drown Lost Boys was no fun. "Smee, my life is over," he said. He reached out with his hook and caught his first mate by the earring.

"Ow!" Smee carefully slid his earring off the hook. "But *mine* isn't. Not yet," he reminded his captain.

Hook went over to the closet. "There'll be no stopping me this time, Smee. Do you hear?" He pulled out a pirate gun and walked to the middle of the room. He cocked the gun and lifted it to his head.

"Oh, not again," Smee said under his breath. This had happened more times than he could remember.

"I say, don't you dare try to stop me this time, Smee. Don't you dare!"

Smee sat looking up at the captain.

Hook's face turned red. What was wrong with his first mate? "I say, you'd better try to stop me," he screamed. "Smee, try to stop me! Smee! Stop me!"

Smee ran to Hook and tried to pull the gun away. It went off with a *pow!* The tiny model of the *Jolly Roger* burst into flames and began to sink into the water tub. "You blithering idiot!" Hook shouted. "Don't you ever frighten me like that again!"

"I'm sorry, Captain. Let's get you to bed."

Smee kicked the ship's wheel. As the wheel spun, Hook's bed came down from the ceiling. Smee helped Hook undress. Each time he took a piece of clothing from the captain, he wrapped it around himself. There was a lot of clothing. Soon Smee looked very large, and Hook looked very small!

"I think a little bit of skulduggery would do you good, Captain," Smee said as he tucked Hook into bed. "Help you take your mind off this Pan business."

Skulduggery? Hook was interested in spite of himself. "What do you mean?"

"First thing in the morning we'll shoot some Indians out of Long Tom." Smee began to fix Hook his "nightcap"—a drink to help the captain get to sleep. "You hate them almost as much as you hate the Lost Boys, don't you?"

"No, no." Hook was tired of killing Indians and Lost Boys. "I want to kill *Pan!*" he raged. "Do you hear me? I want to kill him!"

"Look on the bright side," Smee said. "At least you get to kill his kids." He added a tiny paper umbrella to Hook's drink.

"Oh, bad form, Smee," Hook said. "To kill the defenseless children of a defenseless foe? You know better than that." In the captain's opinion, if you couldn't do a thing with good form, you might as well not do it.

"Wait a minute!" Smee cried. "Lightnin' just struck my brains!"

"That must've hurt," Hook said. He hadn't seen any lightning.

Smee meant that he had had an idea. "Pan's kids!" he said with a gleeful laugh. "We'll make them love you!"

"No little children love me," Hook said indignantly. Had Smee gone crazy?

"That's just the point," the first mate insisted. "It's the ultimate challenge. Pan's kids in love with Hook! Can you imagine his face when he sees his kids standing beside you? Ready to fight for the sleaziest sleaze of the Seven Seas— Captain James Hook!"

Hook picked up his drink. He considered the idea. Could it work? "You know, Smee, I like it," he said finally.

"You'd make a very fine daddy, sir," Smee assured him. He stuck a piece of cork on the tip of the cruel-looking hook. It wouldn't do for the captain to accidentally puncture himself during the night. Then he reached under the pillow and handed the captain his teddy bear. The bear had a hook on its left arm just like its owner. Hook patted the top of the bear's head.

"Teddy," he told it. "I've just had a *lovely* idea. I will not only destroy Pan, but I'll have his own children—I mean, *my* own children—lead the battle!"

By now Smee was wearing all of Hook's clothes, even his dashing red pirate coat. He carefully removed the captain's long black wig and placed it on his own head. Then he sat down in front of the big mirror and admired himself.

" 'Tis the wickedest, prettiest plan *I've* ever heard," he said.

In the bed, Captain James Hook, ruthless pirate, snuggled up to his teddy bear and began to snore.

9. Papa Hook

Jack and Maggie sat uncomfortably behind two small desks. Captain Hook's cabin had been transformed into a classroom. This was the cruelest part yet, Jack thought. Being kidnapped was bad. Being hung from a net on a pirate ship was worse. But being forced to go to school during vacation was *really* mean!

"Now pay attention, class—we have a lot to go over." Captain Hook pointed to an old-fashioned chalkboard. " 'Why Parents Hate Their Children,' " he read.

Maggie raised her hand at once. "Our parents don't hate us," she said defiantly. "Mommy reads to us every night because she loves us very much!"

"She said the 'L-word,' didn't she?" Hook whispered disapprovingly to Smee. "It gives me the shudders! No, I don't think so, child," he said to Maggie. "I think your mother reads you stories every night in order to lull you into sleep so she and Daddy can sit down for three measly minutes without your mindless, inexhaustible, unstoppable, nagging demands. 'He took my toy!' 'She hit my bear!' 'I want a cookie!' I want, want, want—me, mine, now! Don't you understand, child?" he thundered at Maggie. "They tell you stories to *shut you up!*"

Maggie looked over at her brother. He had a thoughtful look on his face. "That's not true, Jack," she said. "He's a liar!"

Suddenly Hook announced a pop quiz. Smee handed a

piece of paper to each child. Then he turned the chalkboard over. Written on the other side was:

Lesson 2.

I LOVE YOU

"What do you think your parents mean when they say 'I love you'?" Hook asked.

Maggie enjoyed quizzes. She stood up on her chair and waved her hand in the air. "I know! I know! They mean we make them really really really really happy all the time."

Hook and Smee leaned their heads together. "Really really really really *wrong!*" they said at the same time.

Wrong? Maggie sat back down in her chair. How could she be wrong?

Abruptly Hook turned and faced her brother. "Jack! Your father went to your sister's school play, but did he show up for your baseball game? No! He missed the most important game on what might have been the most important day of your young life." He brought his big face down very close to Jack's. "Isn't that right?"

Jack thought it over. Suddenly Maggie jumped up and grabbed Hook's hook. "He loved my school play!" she shouted. "You're a dirty old Hook! Jack, help me! Fight for me!"

Jack knew his sister's behavior would only cause more trouble. "Quit it! Let go of him!" he told her. "Have you gone crazy? He's gonna lock you up!"

"She's just a little cranky," Hook told Jack. "Probably missed her nap." To Smee he growled, "Get her out of here!"

Smee picked Maggie up and carried her out of the cabin.

It was Pirates' Prison for this one! Jack could still hear her
yelling from outside: "You've got to remember, Jack! Remember Mommy! Daddy! Home!"

The room was quiet now. Hook walked up to Jack, who
was looking out the door.

"Jack, Jack," the old scoundrel said, "I think you and I
have a lot in common." He put his arm around the boy and
brought him over to a large treasure chest sitting on the floor.
Hook lifted the lid on the chest. It was full of baseball cards!

"Wow . . ." Jack reached in and took a handful of cards.

"You can be anything you want on *my* team, Jack." Hook
knelt next to Jack and patted him lightly on the head with his
hook. "It's all up to you . . . son."

10. Practice Makes Pan

The Lost Boys had become Peter's personal trainers.

They began by having him jog. While he ran through the seasons of the Neverforest, Tink jogged in place on his shoulder. The boys shouted in rhythm like marine sergeants to keep Peter going.

Later it was time for the exercise machines. He did chin-ups while two Lost Boys weighted him down. They held rocks on their laps to make themselves even heavier. He did leg lifts. When he slowed down his repetitions, the boys dangled poison never-ivy above his face. "Don't let that stuff touch your skin!" they warned him. "Never-ivy makes you itch in places you can't scratch!"

Then it was massage time. Peter lay across a giant tree stump as fifteen Lost Boys prodded, pushed, and pummeled his flabby flesh.

Peter was getting tired of it all. He knew he was in terrible shape, but how was all this work going to help him get his children back?

Pockets explained it to him: "The only way to be a kid is to look like a kid."

They had Peter take off his shirt. The Lost Boys thought he looked like a gorilla. First they shaved all the hair on his chest off. Then they mixed up a big batch of war paint. Peter laughed nervously as the boys dabbed streaks of paint on his body. He still couldn't see how this was going to help his kids. "What do I have to do now?" he asked Thud Butt.

Thud Butt's wide face split in a grin. "Now it's time to fly!"

They brought Peter to a cliff. Down below was a mud puddle. Half the Lost Boys stood around the puddle with big signs. They were cue cards for Peter to read as he tried to fly. Some of them said: THINK HAPPY THAWTS, KANDEE, BERFDAY, HORSEY, BUGS. The Lost Boys obviously didn't care much about proper spelling.

Peter's first try was a disaster. He thought of a successful business deal he had made. His feet stayed firmly on the ground. The boys put a helmet on his head and told him to try a run-shot. Peter trotted back into the basketball court. He came running out, slipped, and fell flat on his face. Too Small ran up to him with a measuring tape. "Distance, eight feet," he announced. "Altitude, two feet. Time of flight, two seconds."

"I think we forgot the pixie dust that time," Don't Ask said.

Thud Butt was looking at his slingshot. He called to the other boys. "I think I have an idea!"

The Lost Boys built a giant slingshot. Peter sat nervously in the middle. At the edge of the Nevertree, a group of boys raised a gigantic net, ready to catch the beginning flier. Others began to pull the giant slingshot back.

"Wait, wait!" Peter called out. "Are you *sure* I'm Peter Pan? What if you're wrong? Shouldn't I have some happy thoughts?"

Tink appeared at his side. "Just one happy thought, Peter," she said. "Just one will make you fly."

Peter thought about it. "Not being in this slingshot would make me very happy," he said.

He thought and thought. He thought of the stock market, and of tricky business deals that had made him lots of money. He thought of fancy limousines with car phones. None of it seemed to make him happy now. He wondered if it ever had.

Tink tried to make suggestions. "Cotton candy," she said.

"Cavity-making pink goo," he told her. "Besides, it reminds me of my Aunt Phyllis's hair."

The Lost Boys were getting impatient. They were tired of holding the slingshot tight. "Don't hurry me," Peter said. "I don't have my happy thought yet!"

"Are you happy in springtime?" Tink asked.

Peter shook his head. "I'm allergic to pollen."

"Summer?"

"Sunburn."

"Christmas?"

"Gifts, bills, credit cards." Peter wasn't getting any happier.

Rufio had been watching the whole thing. He moved to the rope that held the slingshot back and drew his sword.

Tink was exasperated. She threw her tiny hands up in the air. "Peter, doesn't *anything* make you happy?"

"Who can be happy under all this pressure?" Peter said. "Just don't rush me!"

Rufio raised his sword into the air and held it with both hands.

"One lousy rotten stinking happy thought," Peter muttered. "How much time do we have left?"

At that moment Rufio brought the sword slashing down

with all his strength. There was a snapping, whooshing sound. Peter sailed screaming into the sky.

"He's going up!" cried one Lost Boy.

Tink covered her eyes with her hand. Then she peeked through. Let him fly! she wished, crossing her fingers and her wings.

"He's coming down!" cried another Lost Boy.

Splat! Peter landed on his backside in the mud puddle. The Lost Boys were crestfallen. They dropped their cue cards and walked away from the puddle.

Later they all gathered for dinner. It was Peter's first meal in Neverland. He was starving after a day of exercise and trying to fly. On one side of the long table sat Rufio and his followers. Tink and her supporters lined the other side. Peter was bruised and banged up. He watched hungrily as steaming covered dishes came out of the big oven at one end of the table. "I've got to eat and build up my strength," he said to the Lost Boy at his side. Another boy set a huge covered platter in front of him. Just then Thud Butt came and sat down on the end of a bench. The other end flew up into the air. The boys all slid down toward Thud Butt. "How many times do we have to tell you—" they yelled. "Don't sit at the end!"

When Thud Butt had found a better seat, everyone clasped hands.

"Everybody say grace," Rufio told them.

"Grace," they all said solemnly.

Then it was time to eat. Peter licked his lips. He took the cover off his platter and leaned forward to see—nothing! What? Weren't they going to serve him? He looked up and down the table. Lost Boys were stuffing their mouths full, wiping their chins, making yummy noises as they ate. But what were they eating? All of the plates on both sides of the table were completely *empty*! Peter was baffled.

All around the table Lost Boys commented to each other about the food. The never-chicken was delicious, the banana splash was wonderful, have you tried the watermelon?

Peter sat with his stomach growling, squinting at rows of empty plates. He leaned over and asked Too Small, "Where's the real food?"

The little boy gave him a look of surprise. "It's everywhere!" he said. "Can't you see it?"

Peter smiled and nodded. He didn't want them to think he was strange, after all. He caught Tink's attention. "Where's the real food?" he whispered to her.

The pixie's mouth seemed to be full. She swallowed before she answered him. "Don't you remember, Peter? This used to be your favorite game."

Rufio laughed at Peter. "He can't do it! He can't imagine food for himself!" He tossed his empty plate across the table.

Peter ducked. "You are a very ill-mannered young man," he told Rufio. "Do you know that?"

An insult. Rufio raised his eyebrows at the challenge. "You're a slug-eating worm," he said.

"Bangarang, Rufio!" some of the Lost Boys yelled.

"You're a very poor role model for these children," Peter said. The Lost Boys booed.

"Slug-slimed sack of rat guts and cat vomit," Rufio answered.

"Bangarang, Rufio!" the boys shouted. They began to keep

score as the insults flew back and forth. Peter gradually got the hang of the game. In the end he won by calling Rufio a list of foul names ending in "paramecium."

"What's a paramecium, Peter?" Don't Ask asked.

Peter pointed to his opponent. *"That*'s a paramecium," he said. "It's a one-celled critter with no brain!" His supporters cheered.

"Don't mess with me," Peter Banning said under his breath. *"I'm* a lawyer!"

He picked up an empty spoon and dipped it into an empty bowl. Then he pulled the top of the spoon back and flicked it at Rufio. A big lump of green and orange goo went *splat* in the middle of Rufio's forehead. It dripped down his face as the Lost Boys went wild with joy. Peter looked down at the spoon. It was covered with goo.

"You're doing it, Peter!" the Lost Boys shouted gleefully. "You're using your imagination!"

Peter turned to look up and down the long table. Everywhere he looked sat plates and bowls filled with delicious, steaming food.

"You're finally playing with us, Peter!" Thud Butt called from the other side of the table. He picked up a roast turkey leg. "Here, catch!"

Peter caught the turkey and bit into it. It was scrumptious! He tossed a baked potato back to Thud Butt. Seconds later, a pie came whizzing toward him. Food started flying left and right, and soon a full-fledged food fight had broken out. Peter hopped up on the table and danced in the middle of it all, laughing and yelling with the others.

Rufio had been watching silently. He was not happy that Peter had learned how to use his imagination. Rufio did not want to give up his position as leader of the Lost Boys—especially not to this fat old imitation Pan.

He picked up a coconut and aimed right at Peter's head. "Hey, Pan-the-Man," he shouted. "Catch this!"

"Peter!" Ace called. "Watch out!" He picked up a sword and tossed it to Peter just as Rufio let go of the coconut. Without thinking, Peter caught the sword in midair and spun around. The sword cut right through the coconut. Two perfectly sliced coconut halves dropped to the table. The Lost Boys stared in amazement. It had all happened so fast!

Peter looked at the sword in his hand. How on earth had he done that? He looked down at the Lost Boys. Could it be true? he wondered. Could it maybe—just possibly—be *true*?

"Bangarang, Peter Pan," Thud Butt whispered.

11. Prove It!

Jack Banning found that living in Pirate Town was like going to a big carnival.

For breakfast, Hook and Smee had brought him to a tavern where they ordered up a huge banana split for him. Later the pirate captain took him fishing, and after that he was allowed to fire off one of the *Jolly Roger*'s big cannons. Jack felt a little guilty. He had been told never to play with guns. But things seemed to be different here in Neverland. The only person who cared what Jack did was Captain Hook himself. And so far Hook had let him do just about anything he wanted.

The best part had come near the end of the day when Hook put Jack in charge of drilling the pirate troops.

"Get moving!" Jack ordered. He was wearing a boy-sized version of Captain Hook's pirate hat. "March in a circle! Faster! Faster!" He clapped his hands. The pirates ran rings around the mainmast of the *Jolly Roger*.

"Halt!" Jack called suddenly. The men all crashed into each other. Jack had to admit he was enjoying his new job. His dad had never let him do anything.

Across the pier from the ship, a little girl stuck her head through the window of Pirates' Prison. "Jack, stop that!" she called. "You're forgetting Mommy and Daddy! We've got to find a way to get out of here!"

Captain Hook walked out on deck and stood by Jack. He turned to scowl in Maggie's direction.

"Who is that loud creature, Jack?" he asked.

Jack said nothing. He was watching the pirates march.

"It's your sister, you dope!" Maggie called across the water.

Jack gave his head a little shake. "That's my sister," he told the captain. He tried hard to remember her name.

Hook and Smee grinned at each other.

Suddenly Jack remembered. "Maggie—her name is Maggie!" He waved to her.

Hook scowled.

"Don't worry, Cap'n," Smee said. "The spell of Neverland is working on him. Two more days and he won't remember anything but you."

"Don't forget us, Jack!" Maggie shouted. Her voice sounded thin and wavery in the twilight. "We've got to get back to Mommy and Daddy! We've got to get home!"

Hook sighed sympathetically. "Try to put behind you all thoughts of home—that place of broken promises," he said.

"What do you mean?" Jack was confused. Wasn't home always a *good* place to be?

Hook smiled his most innocent smile. He reached into his pocket with his hook and brought out Jack's prize baseball. "Jack, son, have I ever made a promise to you that I haven't kept?"

Maggie's throat was sore from so much yelling. She had been put to work in the jail all day, counting Hook's treasure with the captive Lost Boys. Now she felt tired and hungry. She wanted her parents. She even missed her forgetful brother. She felt a tug on her sleeve and ducked her head back through the bars. One of the little Lost Boys was looking at her. He had a strange expression on his face.

"What's a 'mommy'?" he asked her.

"A mommy?" Maggie looked at the other slaves. "Don't any of you remember your mothers?" she asked. No one answered. She picked up one little boy's raggedy pillow. She fluffed it and turned it over for him. "Mommies are the cool side of a pillow when you flip it over."

The slavekids all crowded close. Maggie sat down in the middle of the little Lost Boys and began to sing a lullaby her mother had taught her. It was a beautiful song about angels and stars. Around her, the little Lost Boys closed their eyes.

High up in the Nevertree, Peter could hear a little of the distant lullaby. He sat on a giant branch and looked out over Pirate Town far below. Thud Butt climbed out and sat next to him.

"Peter, can I talk to you?"

"Sure, Thud Butt."

"I remember Tootles," the large boy said.

Peter was amazed. "How could you know Tootles?" he asked. "Was he here?"

"He was a Lost Boy just like us," Thud Butt replied with a nod. "Look—these are his marbles." He put a small pouch into Peter's hand. "They were his happy thoughts. He lost them."

Peter gave a sad laugh. Old Tootles really had lost his marbles.

"Peter, you know what? Maybe my happy thought will help you to fly."

"What's your happy thought, Thud?"

Thud Butt looked left and right. Then he whispered in Peter's ear. "My mother."

"That's nice," Peter said. Then he heard the far-off lullaby again. "Listen," he said. He frowned, trying to recognize the beautiful song.

"It sounds like Wendy," Thud Butt said softly, thinking of the only mother he could remember.

Morning came quickly. Neverland's three suns rose high in the sky. Peter and Rufio stood in the forest with their swords raised. Peter had the feeling he had already lost some weight and gained back a little speed, but he still didn't feel confident where swordplay was concerned.

"Take it easy on me," he begged. "I'm a beginner."

Rufio didn't believe that. "Yeah, right," he said. "I saw the coconut!"

Peter still couldn't figure out how he had split that coconut. It must have been a reflex. Whatever it had been, he doubted he could manage it again.

The lesson began. Rufio lunged at Peter. *Snip!* Rufio's sword cut through Peter's left suspender. The Lost Boys warned Peter to be careful.

"Okay, Gramps," Rufio taunted him. "Give me your best shot."

As Peter charged forward Rufio slipped around behind him. Peter's sword ran right into the ground and stuck there. *Snip!* Rufio cut his right suspender. Peter turned around. "That's so unfair of you!" he protested.

Rufio lifted his sword into the air. Then he crowed at the top of his lungs.

Peter attempted to crow, too. This time he managed a cry like a baby parakeet's.

"Bangarang!" the Lost Boys shouted.

Peter charged forward a second time. *Thunk!* His sword went firmly into the ground again. Rufio swiped with his own sword. Peter's pants fell to the ground. The Lost Boys cried foul. Rufio wasn't fighting fair!

Peter yanked his sword out of the ground and pulled up his pants with his other hand. The fight continued. Peter swung three times at Rufio, missing each time. On the fourth swing sparks flew as Rufio stopped Peter's sword in midair. Suddenly Rufio's sword point was at Peter's neck. The two fighters stood still. Peter stuck out his tongue and made a silly face at Rufio. The dark-skinned boy dropped his sword in disgust.

"Ya can't fly," he said scornfully, "ya can't fight, and ya really can't crow!"

Pockets rose to Peter's defense. "That's not fair! How could he crow? He hasn't done nuttin' to make hisself proud yet!"

Rufio pretended to consider this. "What could the fat man do?" he asked slyly.

"Lots of t'ings," Pockets said. "He could swallow fire."

The other Lost Boys began to chime in. "He could swing on a vine with his teeth!" one suggested. "He could eat more than Thud Butt!" said another.

Pockets was trying to think of something that would make Peter *really* proud. "He could go into Pirate Town and steal Hook's hook!" he exclaimed.

"Yeah! Steal Hook's hook!" The Lost Boys all liked that one. What better way for Peter to prove his Pan-hood?

Rufio smiled a secret smile as the others began to discuss

strategy. Maybe, just maybe, this really was the legendary Pan. If so, stealing the captain's hook was the best way for him to prove it. But Rufio had a feeling that this preposterous imposter would never return from Pirate Town. And that was just fine with him.

12. Past and Present

Tick, tick, tick . . .

Hook awakened slowly. He had been having a lovely dream about shooting Lost Boys out of cannons. But something had disturbed him. He lay in bed for a moment wondering what it was.

Tick, tick, tick . . .

Ticking?

Hook's eyes popped open.

Ticking?

Hook leaped out of bed. He turned this way and that. Ticking meant only one thing to Captain James Hook. "A clock!" he gasped under his breath as he raced up and down his bedroom. "The croc!"

Hook checked under the bed, looked in the closet, stuck his head out the nearest porthole. Nothing.

He threw open the cabin door and dashed out on deck. The steady ticking drew him like a magnet.

Hook tiptoed up to where Jack was sleeping peacefully in a hammock.

He reached his hook into the boy's pocket and brought out a shiny gold pocket watch.

Tick, tick, tick . . .

The sound was maddening. The captain raised his deadly hook just as Jack opened his eyes.

Then Smee appeared. The first mate cupped the watch in both hands to muffle the sound. "Oh, Cap'n," he said cheerfully, "the little elf didn't know any better, now, did he?"

Hook slowly lowered his arm. Smee was right. It would be bad form to skewer a guest for breaking a rule. Especially a rule the guest hadn't even known about. Hook caught the watch on his hook again and hoisted it into the air. "To the museum at once!" he cried.

Hook and Smee led Jack to the Clock Museum, which sat just beyond the giant Croc Tower. Inside was a collection of beautiful and rare old timepieces. All of their faces had been smashed in to make sure they wouldn't start ticking again.

Hook got an idea. He invited Jack to smash his father's pocket watch. "Go on," he said, holding out a big hammer. "You know you want to."

Jack hesitated. Then he remembered being hoisted up in the net while his father watched. He remembered his father trying to buy them back from Hook with his stupid checkbook. He remembered Peter frozen with fear on the mast. He took the hammer. "This is for making me act like a grown-up, but treating me like a child!" he said, hitting the watch square in the face." *Blam!*

"Good form!" Hook cried.

Jack left the battered little pocket watch and walked to a big old clock. "This is for never, never playing next to open windows!" he hollered, and brought the hammer down in the center of the clock face. *Crash!* He turned the table over and laughed as a dozen clocks fell to the floor. "And *that's* for always making promises and then breaking them," he said with satisfaction.

Four ugly, menacing, and very strange-looking pirates came walking into Pirate Town. They walked as if they were very drunk. Actually, three of them were not pirates at all, and they were definitely not drunk. They were nine Lost Boys, three to a man, swaying on one another's shoulders. The shortest of the four was Peter. All of them were made up in the finest rags.

The fake pirates stopped short when they reached the town square. There had been a few changes since their last visit. The Croc Tower had been turned into a scoreboard, and the square itself was now a baseball diamond, with bleachers in the outfield and jeweled satin pillows serving as the bases. Captain Hook applauded from the stands.

Behind the bleachers, Peter helped divide the ugly pirates up into Lost Boys again. They sneaked in behind the seats and spied on their victim. Hook was screwing a special baseball glove attachment onto his left arm. As they watched, he set his regular hook aside on one of the bleachers.

"Look, there it is!" Thudbutt pushed Peter forward. The hook was in easy reach of his hand. "Steal it and crow!"

Peter was still wearing his pirate disguise. He climbed boldly up into the bleachers and sat right next to Hook.

Hook stood up and threw out the first ball. Smee strutted out to the pitcher's mound.

Everyone's eyes were glued to the field. Peter reached out for the hook. He looked up just as his son stepped up to the batter's box.

"Jack, Jack, he's our man!" the pirates chanted.

Peter froze. Jack? Playing on Hook's team? He settled back in his seat to watch the game, the captain's hook forgotten.

"This is for all the games your daddy missed," Hook

shouted to Jack. *"I'd* never miss a single one!"

Jack waved at him. "This one's for you, Captain!"

Smee wound up and threw the ball. It was a vicious curve. There's no way he'll hit that, Peter thought.

Crack! Jack's bat connected, and the ball sailed right out of the park. Peter was stunned. The ball soared like a meteor across the sky of Neverland.

Hook jumped to his feet. The old pirate's eyes showed real pride as he watched the ball. Then he leaped down from the bleachers. He and Jack slapped their right palms together. Smee put Jack on his shoulders. The pirates paraded Jack around the field, cheering and celebrating.

Peter Banning got to his feet in the stands. Feeling numb and cold inside, he stumbled to the ground and walked toward the edge of town. The Lost Boys ran out from under the bleachers to meet him. He walked on past them. He removed his pirate disguise, throwing pieces of it on the ground as he went.

The Lost Boys stood watching Peter for a few moments. Then they shrugged their shoulders in disgust and walked away.

Peter wandered through the Neverforest. His mind was buzzing with strange thoughts.

"Gotta fly," he said to himself. He jumped up into the air and fell to the ground with a thud. "Gotta fly for Jack." He tried again, and again he fell down. "Happy thought," he muttered. "Gotta have one big happy thought." He climbed a tall rock and got ready to jump. Then he looked at the distance below him. "I can't," he murmured. He climbed back down with a sigh. "I just can't."

Just then Jack's baseball came sailing into view. It was still going! *Pow!* The ball struck Peter on the head and knocked him down. Dazed, Peter crawled toward the edge of a nearby pond. Looking for the ball, he caught a glimpse of his own reflection. In the pool he didn't see Peter Banning, attorney-at-law. The face that stared back at him was that of a mischievous boy, hair wild and face full of wonder and adventure. It looked a lot like Jack.

Peter reached into the water and pulled out the baseball. He stood and looked around, bouncing the ball in his palm. He saw his shadow, cast large against the rockface by the biggest of the three suns. Suddenly the shadow spread its feet wide and put its hands on its hips. It threw back its head as if it were about to crow all by itself. Nodding its head, it beckoned Peter to follow it to the giant Nevertree. The shadow pointed toward a knothole in the tree, mostly hidden by vines and leaves.

Peter reached forward and tore away the vines. The knothole was the mouth of a large face carved into the tree. He rose slowly to his feet. As his mind filled with memories, his eyes filled with tears.

The knothole suddenly popped open. Peter climbed in headfirst. It was a tight fit. He squeezed through and found himself in a fantastic place.

The large room looked like it had been carved into the very center of the Nevertree. Pieces of broken furniture lay here and there, and fat mushrooms grew up out of the cluttered floor.

Tink was waiting for him. She sat in a small rocking chair near the center of the room. Her gown was long and flowing. She looked beautiful.

"Welcome home," Tink said.

"Home . . ." Peter looked around again. Tink began to glow brighter and brighter, lighting up the whole room so Peter could see it clearly. There were rows of little beds at one end of the room and a big table in the middle. The other end had a great old fireplace that was large enough for a boy to walk inside. Everything had been smashed and broken, and all the wood was charred.

More memories poured into Peter's head. "What happened here?" he asked Tink in a quiet voice.

"Hook happened. The pirates got in and burned it when you didn't come back," she told him.

Peter walked around, picking up small objects here and there. He found a thimble on the floor. "This is Wendy's house," he said. "The Home Underground. Tootles and Nibs built it for her. I remember—" His eyes widened as he realized what he was saying. "I *remember*," he whispered, growing more and more excited as it all began to fall into place. "Wendy used to sit and tell us stories in that chair—only it wasn't there, it was right here." He pointed to the floor near the fireplace. "We'd come back from adventures and she would darn our socks. Tink, your little apartment was right here. Michael slept here in his basket bed. And John slept in this bunkbed."

There was a little stuffed animal lying half under one of the beds. It was dirty and charred from the fire. Peter picked it up and cradled it in his arms. "Taddy, my Taddy . . ." He looked up at Tink. "My mother used to put him in the pram to keep me company. I remember my mother. . . ." He fell silent.

"Yes," Tink said. "What else?"

"I remember her voice . . . talking about how I'd grow up . . . go to fine schools . . . work in an office . . ." Peter spoke slowly. He hugged the stuffed bear to his chest.

"Isn't that what all grown-ups want for their children?" Tink asked him.

"But I was afraid," Peter said. "I didn't want to grow up—to grow old and die. I crawled out of my pram. And you found me, Tink. You taught me how to fly, and we came to Neverland." He looked sad. "When I went back home for a visit, Mother had forgotten about me. I looked in the window and saw her with a new baby boy. Then I found other windows to visit, ones that weren't closed. I left my shadow in Wendy's nursery, and I came back to find it. That's how I met her. She heard me crying when I couldn't stick the shadow back on." Peter's eyes got a faraway look in them. "I came back many times for Wendy in the spring. But she kept getting older. Then the last time, I found her in a rocking chair by the fire. She looked different. She told me she'd forgotten how to fly. She told me she was ever so much older than twenty. She showed me her own grand-daughter, Moira." Peter sighed. "Moira. After I saw Moira, I couldn't leave. I stayed with Wendy. But it meant I had to grow up. I had to go to school. . . ."

Tink was watching Peter. "I can see why you have trouble flying," she said softly. "How can you find a happy thought among so many sad memories?"

Peter felt as if he wanted to cry. He turned away from the room with all of its memories. He tossed the little stuffed bear up into the air. It turned end over end. Peter caught the bear and looked at it again. He was remembering his own father, holding him, playing with him. He blinked his eyes. Then he remembered holding Jack. He remembered how he used to play with Jack and Maggie before he had become too busy with work and life. He closed his eyes, watching the past. He remembered his wife, Moira, and the joy he had found in being part of a family.

"Tink!" he cried. "My family—my wonderful, incredible family. I did it! I did it! I found my happy thought!"

Peter opened his eyes. Then he looked down. He was fifteen feet above the floor of the cave. Tink was hovering in the air below him.

"I'm flying!" he called out, half-delighted and half-alarmed. "Flying!" He started to fall. The floor of the cave rushed up toward him.

"Hold that happy thought!" Tink yelled from right beneath him. She was about to get flattened! Peter closed his eyes and concentrated. He floated to a stop inches above the floor. The little faerie breathed a sigh of relief.

"Follow me now, and all will be well," she told him. "It's time for you to fly solo!"

They flew like birds out of the Home Underground. Peter caught up to Tink in the branches of the Nevertree. He was laughing and crowing at the same time. He dove through the air like a divebomber. He stitched like a needle through the fluffy clouds. He raced the wind and leaped on its back.

Down below he saw a council of war. The Lost Boys were plotting an attack on Pirate Town to win back their captured friends. Suddenly the great bell that hung high in the branches of the Nevertree started ringing. All the boys looked up.

Peter appeared, flying circles around the Nevertree. The Lost Boys gathered below, staring up in astonishment. Gone was the fat old man Tink had dragged into their midst. Gone was the man with no imagination, the lawyer who had forgotten how to play. "Peter! Peter! You're doing it!" they cried. "You're doing it!"

Peter flew toward the waterfall. He turned in midair and headed back toward the Nevertree. When he reached the tree, he did a flip and flew straight for Rufio. He took out his knife. *Snick!* Rufio stood frozen as Peter sliced his belt neatly in two. His pants fell down around his ankles. The Lost Boys laughed uproariously.

Peter threw the knife away. He did another flip. Then he started swimming through the air: first a crawl, then a backstroke, then like a frog. He shot over to the basketball court and started to dribble a basketball in midair.

Meanwhile Rufio raced past the mud pond and ducked into his hut. He had a strange gleam in his eyes. He grabbed the Pan sword and ran out of the hut.

Peter was playing a wild game of basketball with the Lost Boys. He flew up to the hoop and slam-dunked the ball.

Suddenly Rufio charged onto the court. He had the sword in his hand. Peter landed in front of him, ready for trouble.

Then Rufio did an amazing thing. He dropped to his knees and turned the sword around so the handle faced Peter. Then he bowed his head.

Peter took the sword and drew a line in the dirt. Rufio got up and crossed the line to stand next to Peter and all the other Lost Boys.

"You are the Pan," he said. "You can fight, you can fly, you can crow."

At that, Peter spread his feet apart and put his hands on his hips. Then he threw his head back and crowed the mightiest crow Neverland had heard in a long, long time.

Peter and Rufio bowed to each other as the Lost Boys cheered. Peter Pan was back!

The celebration went on for hours into the night. The Lost Boys whooped and danced around great bonfires. In the air above them, Peter demonstrated acrobatic flying stunts.

"Oh, the cleverness of me!" he yelled, whirling like a cyclone through the air. Then he noticed something. Tink was not part of the celebration. Peter flew up to the Nevertree and landed with a flip in front of her miniature house. He peered in the window.

"Hey, Tink, you're missing all the fun!" he said.

Tink was sitting on a little stool made from a spool of thread.

"Peter," she asked, "do you remember how you saved Tiger Lily from Hook and made peace with the Indians?"

"Sure," Peter said. What was wrong with Tink? Of course he remembered. "Oh, the cleverness of me," he said. "We've had the best adventures, haven't we?"

Tink's tiny face was serious. "And do you remember your next great adventure? The one to save your own kids from Captain Hook?"

Peter got a funny look on his face. "Kids?" he whispered. "Peter Pan's got kids?"

"Peter, why are you in Neverland?" Tink asked him.

That was an easy question. He was here to be a Lost Boy and fight pirates. And to fly, of course. "Because I always want to be a little boy and have fun," he said. "C'mon, ask me another one. I like this game!"

Abruptly colored lights began to flash and smoke came

from Tink's house. Peter backed away in alarm. Was it on fire, like the Home Underground?

There was a smashing, crashing sound. Then Peter blinked in amazement. A full-size, woman-size Tink stood before him. What was left of the roof of her little house sat on top of her head like a funny hat. But Tink didn't look funny. She looked serious. And she looked beautiful.

"Tink," Peter said softly, "look what you did."

"This is the only wish I've ever made just for myself," Tink told him. "It's the biggest feeling I've ever felt, and this is the first time I've been big enough to feel it." Then she took him into her arms and gave him a kiss. "I love you, Peter Pan," she whispered.

Peter felt very strange. "I love—" Then he paused. "I love her," he finished.

Tink was confused. "Her—who?" she asked.

"I love Moira," Peter said firmly. It was all starting to come back to him now. "And Jack and Maggie." He pushed away from the expanded pixie in alarm. "Jack and Maggie—we have to save them! Come on, Tink, let's go!"

Tink was crushed. "And when it's all over, you'll leave and never come back again," she said sadly.

Peter knew it was true. He and Tink looked into each other's eyes for a long moment.

Then the faerie gave her head a little shake. "Well, what are you waiting for?" she said. Her eyes were full of sorrow, but she was smiling at him. "Go on—save them, Peter!" She blew a burst of pixie dust at him, and he darted up into the Neverland sky. A great red sun was rising out of the water.

With tears in her eyes, Tink watched as Peter Pan turned and flew off into the dawn.

13. Pandemonium

Jack Banning stood next to his friend Captain Hook on the deck of the *Jolly Roger*. The other pirates were crowded around them. Jack and Hook were dressed exactly alike, from their polished black boots to their tall captain's hats. Hook was giving Jack his very first pirate's earring. It was made of gold and looked just like a miniature hook.

Suddenly a loud crowing sound came from high in the sky. Jack looked up. The shadow of Peter Pan was on the mainsail.

Then a sword point appeared through the sail. *Rip-rip-rip* . . . Someone was cutting the outline of the shadow right through the canvas. The cutout fell to the deck. Smee walked over and picked it up. His eyes grew wide when he recognized the outline. He dropped the cutout with a squeak of fear and ran off to find a hiding place.

Then Peter Pan was standing in the opening in the sail. Jack blinked up at him in amazement. Did he know this large boy? There was something familiar about him. . . .

"Peter Pan!" Hook called. "Has it been three days already? Time flies!"

Peter leaped through the hole in the sail and zoomed down to the deck. He made a fantastic flip in the air and landed to face the evil captain with a smile on his lips. "Hand over my children now, codfish, and you and your men go free," he said.

"Why don't you ask the boy yourself?" Hook said. He patted Jack on the shoulder. "Someone here to see you, *son*."

Peter winced. He hated to see the captain touch Jack. "Jack, take my hand," he told his son. "We're going to go home now."

"Home?" Jack moved closer to the captain. What was this strange boy talking about? "I *am* home," he said.

"Good form!" Hook said with a laugh. "You see, Peter, Jack is *my* son now." He shoved the boy to one side and raised his hook to Peter. "I've waited a long time to shake your hand with this, Peter Pan!" he snarled. "Prepare to meet thy doom!" He reached for his sword.

"Dark and sinister man, have at thee!" Peter called. He did a flip down the steps to the main deck. Pirates dropped down out of the rigging all around him, weapons drawn.

The battle began as the pirates attacked from all directions. Peter flew out of their grasp quick as a sparrow, then returned to send them hurtling. *Wham! Smash!* The pirates knocked over crates and crashed into one another. Drawing his sword, Peter spun around in a circle, taking them all on at the same time.

Jack watched the fight from the upper deck next to Captain Hook. His eyes were on Peter. "Don't I know him, Captain?" he asked.

"No," Hook lied with a shake of his head. "You've never seen him before in your life!"

"Jack!" Peter called up to his son as he continued the fight. "You won't believe this, but I found my happy thought! It took me three days, but I finally found it and up I went. You know what my happy thought was, son? It was *you*!" Peter flew up into the air. "You and Mommy and Maggie!"

Hook was furious. He had to stop this sickening reunion.

He darted toward the rope that held a heavy net high above the deck. Jack saw him slash at it with his hook. The boy's eyes opened wide.

"Dad! Look out!" he cried.

Peter stopped in midair. "What did you call me?"

"Dad, you're my dad," Jack said as the net fell on top of Peter. He sounded like someone who was waking out of a deep sleep. "I thought you hated to fly."

Eager pirates pulled Peter down onto the deck. He struggled to rise. It was no use. He was caught in the heavy net.

"Bangarang!" Peter called.

"Uh-oh," said a pirate.

"Bangarang!" came a chorus of voices as another ship pulled into view alongside the *Jolly Roger*. The new ship was called the *Dark Avenger*, and its decks were swarming with Lost Boys. With Rufio in the lead, they swung and leaped onto Hook's ship. The pirates moved to meet them with swords and guns. The boys countered with odd-looking homemade weapons. They were quick and clever, and they ran rings around the slow pirates.

Rufio fought his way to Peter's side and freed him from the net. The two crowed together, then they turned back-to-back and fought the pirates.

Smee darted out to ring the bell on the upper deck. He was calling for reinforcements. "Help!" he shouted. "I don't want to die. I don't hate anybody. In fact, I don't even dislike anybody. I don't think I want to be a pirate anymore. I've got a mother at home!"

The fighting stopped as the two armies formed lines facing each other. "Get ready. . . ." Peter told the Lost Boys. He raised his arm.

"Charge!" shouted Hook. The pirates surged forward.

"Now!" Peter yelled, dropping his arm.

The Lost Boys held up mirrors as the pirates charged them. Blinded by the reflected sunlight, the pirates began to bump into each other. They stumbled around the deck, cursing and swinging their swords at the empty air.

"Next plan!" Peter called. "Jack, watch this one! We'll show 'em who's chicken!"

Ace and Thud Butt leaped onto the *Jolly Roger*. They had a strange machine with them. It looked a little like a machine gun, but it had a cage on top of it. In the cage were some very nervous-looking chickens. The boys aimed the weapon and pulled the trigger. There was a loud clucking and squawking sound as *eggs* shot out of the gun. *Splat! Splatter!* Pirates reeled about the deck, eggs and eggshells dripping from their faces. Jack stood on the sidelines, watching in amazement.

Hook was horrified. Nothing was going right. "Smee!" he called out to his first mate. "Help! Do something intelligent!"

Smee thought for a moment. Then he ducked into the main cabin and locked the door behind him. What could be more intelligent than finding a safe place to hide?

Now the boys brought out their tomato guns. Pirate reinforcements were heading up the tunnel from Pirate Square. As they rushed out onto the pier they were met with volleys of gooey tomatoes. *Splish! Squish!*

On board the ship, Thud Butt was in the thick of the fighting. Curling himself into a ball, he rolled down a flight of stairs and bumped a bunch of pirates right into an open hatchway! As he stood up, another group of cutthroats surrounded him, and he called for help from the Lost Boys.

Jack was tired of watching from the sidelines. Grabbing a

nearby rope, he launched himself toward Thud Butt and knocked the threatening pirates to either side.

"Thanks!" Thud Butt said to his rescuer. "Who are you?" Before Jack could answer, Thud Butt was called to assist the other Lost Boys at the tunnel. The large boy hurried off, ready to become the Thudball again at a moment's notice.

Peter had lost track of Jack in the confusion. He ran this way and that, fighting pirates as he searched. The Lost Boys had started to overpower the pirates. Fighting spilled onto the pier as the boys forced their enemies off the ship.

Rufio had climbed to the upper deck to challenge Captain Hook. Peter raced up the steps just as the fight was about to begin. "No," he told his new friend. "Hook is mine!"

Suddenly Peter heard a familiar voice calling through the sounds of battle. He looked around and saw Maggie leaning through the window of Pirates' Prison. His daughter was in danger! Forgetting his enemies, Peter flew up from the deck and headed for the prison.

Inside the jail, Maggie and the slavekids were working on an escape plan when the jailer burst in on them. The huge pirate picked Maggie up and started to drag her into another room. Suddenly Peter Pan raced into the room with his sword drawn. He quickly overpowered the jailer and swept his daughter up into his arms. "I missed you," he told her. "I love you so much!"

Lost Boys crowded into the jail cell. "This is why we're fighting," Peter told them proudly. "This is my daughter, Maggie. I want you to defend her with your lives while I go get Jack." He saluted the Lost Boys with his sword and took off back toward the ship. The boys crowded curiously around Maggie.

"Are you a girl?" Latchboy asked her.

Maggie slapped her forehead in disbelief.

Back on the ship, Thud Butt was leading the attack. On the upper deck Hook and Rufio fought with swords while Jack watched anxiously. The battle was close, with first one fighter and then the other in control. Finally Rufio lifted his sword over his head in both hands.

"Well, looky, looky—I got Hooky!" he crowed.

"Sadly, you have no future as a poet," the treacherous Hook told him. Suddenly he leaped forward. Rufio looked down with surprise as the pirate's sword passed through his body. He fell to the deck.

Just then Peter landed next to Rufio. He knelt down and cradled his friend's head in his lap. Rufio looked up and saw Jack watching them. "You know what I wish?" he asked Peter. "I wish I had a dad like you." Then he closed his eyes for the last time.

Shocked, Jack turned to Captain Hook. "He's only a boy, just like me," he said angrily. "Bad form, Captain!"

Peter got to his feet and walked toward the evil pirate.

"Are you ready for me, Peter?" Hook snarled.

"Dad!" Jack rushed to his father's side and hugged him. "I want to go home." He removed his miniature pirate hat and tossed it at the captain.

Hook was furious. "Where are you going?" he cried as Peter lifted his son into his arms.

"Home!" Peter called. He leaped into the air and flew down to where the Lost Boys waited on the wharf.

14. Peter Prevails

Hook shook with rage on the upper deck as his hated enemy flew away. "Peter Pan, I'll always be your worst nightmare come true!" he shouted. "Come back and kill me now, or I'll be back. There will be more daggers bearing notes signed JAS. Hook. I'll fling daggers in the doors of your children's children's children's children!" he vowed bitterly.

Inside Hook's cabin, Mister Smee filled a large bag with as much of the captain's treasure as he could carry. Someone might as well benefit from all this loot, he told himself.

Down on the wharf, the pirates had continued to retreat from their enemies. Finally defeated, they dropped their swords and let the Lost Boys take them all prisoner. "Bangarang!" shouted the victorious Lost Boys.

Peter and Jack landed on the wharf. Maggie ran to her father and brother with a cry of joy. The Lost Boys surrounded their leader as he embraced his children. Thud Butt called for a big victory banquet back at the Nevertree, and there were more shouts of "Bangarang." Then Latchboy noticed that one of the boys was missing.

"Where's Rufio?" he asked.

Peter told the sorrowful boys about their brave comrade as they headed into the tunnel toward Pirate Square.

Captain Hook still stood fuming on the deck of the *Jolly*

Roger. "I haven't finished with you yet, Peter Pan!" he bellowed. "Come back, do you hear me?"

Maggie looked up at the nasty old man. "You need a mommy very, very badly," she called back to him.

Hook refused to give up. He scrambled down from the upper deck and charged toward the gangplank. "Peter! Peter!" he shouted. "Wherever you go, wherever you are, I'll find you."

Peter had had enough. He gave the kids a big hug. Then he turned and walked back to the bottom of the gangplank. He faced the dreaded Captain Hook. "What do you want?" he asked quietly.

"I want you." Hook made a slashing motion with his hook. "Just you."

Peter thought for a moment. Hook was right. It had to be finished now, once and for all, or it would never be over. He drew his sword. "You got me, old man." Then he threw back his head and crowed.

Swift as an arrow, Peter flew up the gangplank. "Peter Pan the Avenger is back!" he announced as he landed in front of the pirate.

The captain wore an evil grin. "And the hook is waiting," he told his enemy.

Sparks flew as the two swords came together.

Jack and Maggie joined the Lost Boys in cheering Peter on as the two foes battled. Some of the boys wanted to help their leader, but Peter motioned them away.

"Put up your swords, boys," he told them. "It's Hook and me this time."

Hook seemed to glow with a new energy. "Prepare to die, Peter," he snarled. "It's the only adventure you have left!"

Their swords met with a loud clanging as the two battled, first on the ship and then on the wharf. Hook's deadliest blows were turned aside by the valiant Peter Pan. Then the nasty captain had a nasty idea.

"You know you're not really Peter Pan, don't you?" he whispered to Peter as they thrust and parried. "This is all a dream! When you wake up, you'll be fat old Peter Banning again—a cold and selfish man who never has time for his wife and children."

Could it be true? Peter was horrified. He hesitated for a split second. Then the Lost Boys rallied to his aid.

"We believe in you!" they called to their leader. "You are the Pan!" Jack and Maggie joined the chorus.

Peter surged with renewed energy. *Clang!* He knocked Hook's sword out of his hand. It hit the ground, and Hook stood at Peter's mercy.

Then Peter slowly bent down and retrieved the fallen sword. Turning it around, he graciously offered it to Hook. As the captain reached to take it, he suddenly lashed out with his razor sharp hook, cutting Peter's arm.

"Bad form!" Jack yelled from the sidelines.

Peter looked up from his bleeding arm. "James," he said, "that was so very unfair of you."

The battle resumed, wilder than ever. Peter forced Hook back through the tunnel and into Pirate Square. Soon the two were dueling by themselves at the base of the thirty-foot-tall Croc Tower.

Then the Lost Boys and Maggie and Jack were suddenly crowding around the combatants, each one holding a loudly ticking clock.

Tick, tick, tick . . .

All Hook could think of was the crocodile that had swallowed his hand. He glanced nervously up at the Croc Tower.

"Tick-tock, tick-tock," Peter taunted him. "Hook's afraid of the old dead croc!" He danced in front of his enemy, easily avoiding the captain's deadliest blows. Hook tried so hard to kill his foe that he got all tangled up in his own coat. Peter reached out with his blade and flipped the wig and hat from his archenemy's head. They flew through the air to drop neatly onto Too Small, who blinked in surprise. Then Peter twirled around and knocked Hook's sword out of his hand. The old pirate fell to his knees. The will to fight seemed to have gone out of him. His eyes fluttered weakly, and he was gasping for breath. Peter placed the point of his sword against his old foe's throat.

"Good form, Peter," Hook whispered. "I am fallen. Please give me back my dignity." He pointed toward the wig that still sat on Too Small's head. "You took my hand. You owe me something."

Peter hated to see anyone suffer. He went to the little Lost Boy and picked up the hat and wig. He tossed the hat away. Then he returned to Hook's side and handed the old man his wig. Hook clutched it gratefully as Peter brought his sword back to the pirate's throat.

"You killed Rufio," Peter said. "You kidnapped my children. You deserve to die."

Hook nodded solemnly. "Strike, Peter Pan," he urged. "Strike true. Finish it."

Then Jack and Maggie ran to Peter's side. They didn't want to see their father kill anybody—not even the evil old captain. They tugged at his sword arm, pulling it away from Hook's throat.

"Daddy, let's go home," Maggie pleaded. "He's just a mean old man without a mommy."

"Yeah," Jack said. "Let's go home. He can't hurt us now."

Slowly Peter lowered the sword.

Hook laughed with relief. "Oh, bless you, child!" he said. "Good form, Jack. After all, what would the world be like without Captain Hook?" He carefully adjusted the wig atop his head.

"I want you to take your ship and go," Peter said sternly to the old man. "And I never want to see your face in Neverland again. Promise?"

Captain Hook nodded in agreement. As Peter turned to walk away, his children at his sides, the crafty old pirate raised his right hand into the air. A long sharp knife slid out of his sleeve and into his palm.

"You fools!" he cried out. "James Hook *is* Neverland!" He jumped to his feet and lunged toward Peter, ramming him back against the Croc Tower as Jack and Maggie looked on in horror.

"You lied," Peter said, struggling to free himself. "You broke your promise!"

Hook laughed and raised his deadly hook. "Whenever children read," he gloated, "it will say 'Thus perished Peter Pan.'"

Suddenly Tink zipped in between the two, once more the size of a proper pixie. She knocked the captain's arm to one side. The gleaming hook sank deep into the belly of the stuffed crocodile with a loud *thunk!*

"Help!" the captain cried. "I'm hooked! I'm hooked!"

Peter stepped away from the Croc Tower as Hook twisted and turned. The tower began to shake and shudder inside its scaffolding. Something was about to happen. Everyone backed away, their eyes on the struggling captain.

Up above, the clock in the croc's gigantic jaws had come loose. It hurtled to the ground behind Hook. Finally the captain wrenched his hook free from the base of the tower. As he backed away, he stumbled over the clock and fell, tangling himself in his fancy vest.

There was a loud snapping sound as the wooden scaffolding around the Croc Tower began to crack and fall to the ground. Hook stared up in shock, crawling on his hands and knees away from the trembling tower.

"Oh, no!" cried the cowering captain. "I want my mommy!"

Then the whole tower swayed and toppled forward. The croc's huge jaws were wide open. The tower landed right on top of Hook with a loud crashing noise, swallowing him whole!

The dust settled slowly. Everyone was silent.

Then Too Small rushed out from behind the other Lost Boys. "He's gone!" he shouted. He ran right through the arch formed by the croc's empty jaws. "Hook's gone!"

Peter took his sword out and held it aloft. "Bangarang!" he yelled. "No more Hook!"

"No more Hook!" the Lost Boys cried. "Hooray for Pan-the-Man!" They crowded excitedly around their hero, all talking at once. Each of the boys had a different idea for their next big adventure.

Peter was standing quietly in the midst of the celebrating Lost Boys. His eyes were on his son and daughter where they stood with Tink. He had a sad smile on his face as he listened to the Lost Boys' plans.

Too Small came to stand in front of him. "What's wrong, Peter?" he asked in his little voice.

"I can't stay and play," Peter told them. "I've done what I came to do, and now I have to go back home."

Tink turned her tiny face away as Peter walked over to Jack and Maggie. The pixie had been dreading this moment. Peter asked her to sprinkle the children with a little faerie dust. Then he held their hands.

"Jack, Maggie, listen to me," he said. "All you have to do is think one happy thought and you'll be able to fly home safely."

One happy thought? Maggie closed her eyes. "Mommy!" she cried.

Peter looked at his son. What would his happy thought be?

Jack smiled proudly at his father. "My Dad . . . Peter Pan!" he said.

Peter looked at his children with love and pride. Then all three Bannings flew into the air, with Tink out in front.

Peter looked down at the ring of Lost Boys watching forlornly on the ground. "Tink!" he called to the little faerie. "You know the way home. I'll be right behind you!" He released the children's hands and flew back to his friends.

The boys were terribly sad as Peter shook hands with each of them. "I won't forget you this time," he promised. "You're all my boys. It's always and forever in Neverland." He stepped back and looked them over carefully. "So who do I leave in charge?"

The Lost Boys lined up in front of him, each one eager for the great honor. Peter paced up and down, then stopped. He held the Pan sword out to Thud Butt. With a huge grin on his face, Thud Butt knelt to receive the sword and the title of Pan.

Peter gave him a big hug. "I want you to take care of everyone who's smaller than you."

"Peter Pan forever!" Thud Butt shouted proudly. The boys all nodded in agreement. Some of them wiped tears from their eyes. No Nap blew his nose.

Peter walked to the center of the square. "Thank you," he said to the Lost Boys. "Thank you all." He looked around, a long last look at the people and the places of his childhood. Then he looked straight up into the sky.

Thud Butt raised the Pan sword into the air. Tears were streaming down his round cheeks. "Bangarang for Pan-the-Man," he yelled.

"Bangarang!" the Lost Boys cried.

Up into the sky flew Peter Pan. He waved once, then headed away from Neverland. The Lost Boys watched until he was a tiny speck.

Too Small wiped the tears from his eyes and smiled. "Wow," he said. "That was a great game!"

15. Peace at Last

The first light of dawn crept through the nursery windows at Number 14 Kensington. Moira Banning sat asleep in the big rocking chair in the middle of the room. A breeze stirred the windows. They opened inward, and a flurry of tropical leaves danced into the room. One of them landed on Moira's shoulder.

Then Jack and Maggie flew through the open windows and landed lightly on the rug. Jack looked around him in a daze. Did he know this place? He looked at Moira.

"I know her," he said.

Maggie hushed him. She was feeling a little sleepy herself. "It's Mom." She walked over to the sleeping woman. "She looks like an angel, doesn't she?" she whipered. "Let's not wake her yet."

The children crawled gratefully into their little beds and snuggled under the covers.

Moira woke up slowly. She plucked the odd-looking leaf from her shoulder with a puzzled look. She rose and crossed to the windows. How had these gotten open? She closed and locked them with a sigh. Turning, she saw two little lumps in the children's beds. She shook her head in disbelief. Funny what tricks the light could play on your eyes.

The nursery door opened, and Granny Wendy came in.

She seemed older than before, and she leaned heavily on her cane as she walked. She looked at the rocking chair. "My dear child," she said to Moira, "have you been up all night?"

Moira turned from the little beds. "I see them so often in my dreams," she said to her grandmother, "that when I wake up, it's as if they're still here."

Maggie popped up in her bed. Granny Wendy's mouth dropped open. Moira turned.

"Mommy!" Maggie cried.

Jack sat up in his bed. "Mom!" he called.

Moira's legs gave way and she sank to the floor. Maggie and Jack hopped out of bed and ran to their mother's side. Moira wrapped her arms around them. She was crying tears of pure joy.

The statue of the boy called Peter Pan stood playing his pipes, forever joyful, forever young, in Kensington Gardens. Near the base of the statue a man lay sprawled in the snow.

Not far away, a grounds keeper was sweeping trash out of the park. His broom swept some empty bottles across the sidewalk. *Tink-tink-tink* went the bottles as they rolled.

The man in the flower bed opened his eyes. "Tink?" he said. "Tink! Tink!"

"Good morning, Peter," said a man's voice.

"Good morning," Peter answered, still half-asleep.

"And how are you this morning?"

"Not bad." Then Peter looked around. There was no one in sight. Who on earth was he talking to?

He lifted himself up on his elbows and blinked in surprise. Smee? How had Smee gotten out of the Neverland? And what was he doing talking to a statue? Peter rubbed his eyes, then looked again. It wasn't Smee after all. It was the grounds keeper, stopping for a chat with the statue of Peter Pan. The old man moved away, and Peter got cautiously to his feet.

As he stepped onto the sidewalk, a tiny figure landed on the statue's shoulder. Peter froze. For a long moment he said nothing. Dreams and memories were all mixed up in his head. Then he stepped forward.

"Tink?"

The little pixie smiled at him. "Say it, Peter—say it and mean it," she begged him.

Peter grinned. "I believe in faeries!" he said. And he meant it with all his heart.

The sun was rising behind the city as Peter looked up at the statue.

"You know that place between asleep and awake?" Tink asked. Her voice was filled with love and hope. "That place where you still remember your dreams? That's the place where I'll always love you, Peter Pan. And that's where I'll be waiting for you when you come back."

Then the sunlight grew brighter. Peter had to shade his eyes and turn his head. When he looked back at the statue, its shoulder was empty.

Peter stood for a minute and frowned at the statue of the boy with his pipes and his expression of joy. Why am I standing out here? he wondered. He looked down at himself. What am I doing standing in Kensington Gardens in the middle of the winter without a coat? He turned and started down the path toward home, shouting as he ran:

"Moira, Maggie, Jack! I'm back! I'm home!"

A little boy making snowballs looked up as Peter did a flip over a car parked along the road. "Not bad for a ninety-two-year-old!" Peter called out. "Happy Christmas!" He bounded up the steps to Number 14 and knocked three times on the door.

"Moira, Maggie, Jack!" he called. He knocked three more times. "Your daddy's back, he's back!" There was no sound from the tall, old house.

He knocked again. "If you're not here, I'll go to the rear!" He jumped up on the narrow ledge by the steps. I could break my neck, he thought, looking down at the sidewalk below. What the heck! He ran down the ledge and jumped over the stone pillar at the bottom. Then he did three flips on the sidewalk. He slipped at the end of the last one and fell down with a laugh. A small pouch popped out of his pocket and marbles spilled all over the sidewalk. He got up on his hands and knees and began to gather them up. The little boy making snowballs just looked at him.

"Lost my marbles," Peter told him. Then he raced to the backyard and did a flip over the wall. Nana was waiting for him, tail wagging.

Suddenly he heard a strange ringing sound. Peter looked confused. "Tink?" he said. He followed the noise to the frozen garden bed. Grabbing a shovel, he dug until he had unearthed a small portable telephone.

He lifted the phone to his face. "Brad, hi!" he said. "How am I? I'm okay, I'm incredible, I'm greater than good! Listen, I'd love to chat, but I've gotta climb a drainpipe right now." He started to put the phone down in the snow. Then he picked it up again and added, "See, I'd fly, but I've run out of faerie dust. . . ." He stuffed the phone into his vest and turned to the drainpipe.

It didn't take long for Peter to pull himself up the drainpipe. He pushed against the big nursery windows. Locked! He pulled himself up onto the ledge below the windows. He looked inside. Through the curtains he saw his family: Wendy, Maggie, Jack, and Moira, tearful but happy! He tapped four times on the glass. "Maggie, Moira, Jack, Granny Wendy!" he sang. "I'm home, I've come back, I'm here!"

Jack climbed up on the windowsill and peered out between the curtains. "Excuse me," he said with a mischievous grin, "do you happen to have an appointment?"

Peter laughed. "Yeah, you little pirate—with you, for the rest of my life!"

Jack unlocked the windows and opened them wide. Peter hopped inside and picked up his son.

"Jack, what have I told you about this window!" he scolded as he spun the boy around. "*Never* close it! Always leave it open!"

Moira was waiting for him in the center of the room. He walked over and gave her a kiss. In the middle of it, the phone began to ring again. Peter reached inside his jacket. "I have to take this call," he told his wife solemnly. "Hello, Brad? Have you ever wondered what it feels like to really fly? Well, it's like this—"

He pulled his arm back and threw the phone out through the open windows.

Moira hugged him tightly. "Where have you been?" she asked.

Maggie ran up before he could answer. "How much do you love me?" she asked as he whirled her up in his arms.

"All the way to infinity and back again," Peter answered truthfully.

Peter heard a cough and turned to see Tootles standing at the nursery door.

"Hullo, Peter," said the sad old man. "I missed the adventure again, didn't I?"

Peter had a flash of memory. He set Maggie down, then walked over to Tootles and handed the old man the pouch filled with marbles. "I think these belong to you," he said.

The old man opened the pouch and poured the brightly colored marbles into his trembling hands. He looked up to where Wendy was standing on the other side of the room. "Look!" he said to her. "I didn't lose my marbles after all."

Granny Wendy smiled tenderly at the delight on the old man's face. She crossed the room and took Peter's hand.

"Hullo, boy," she said to him.

"Hullo, Wendy-lady," Peter said back to her. "Give us a squdge." He gave her a big hug.

Granny Wendy looked at Peter's face. "Boy, why are you crying?" she asked him.

"I don't know." Peter shook his head. "It's just a tear for every happy thought."

"And one for me?" Wendy asked.

"And me?" Jack said.

"And me?" Maggie added.

"And one for me, too," old Tootles said from beside the open window. He tilted the pouch and poured a small amount of sparkling dust onto the top of his head. As the family watched in amazement the old man began to rise slowly into the air.

"Thank you!" Tootles called to Peter. "Good-bye!" He spun in the air and flew gracefully out the window, on his way back to Neverland at last.

Peter, Moira, Jack, Maggie, and Granny Wendy all ran to the window. They leaned against the railing and waved farewell to Tootles.

Wendy cocked her head at her favorite orphan. Peter Banning's eyes sparkled like a child's as he watched the old man rise above the rooftops of London.

"So, Peter," she said to him. "Your adventures are over."

Peter reached out his arms and drew his family in close to him. "Oh, no," he said. "To live will be an awfully big adventure!"

About the Author

Geary Gravel is the author of several science-fiction novels, including the *Fading Worlds* adventures. He has worked as a sign-language interpreter for the Deaf since 1977. He is patiently waiting for a good reason to grow up.